A lethal package

There was something decidedly sexy about competence, Kaylie reflected idly. For one short, awful moment she thought she'd said the words aloud. They were totally unexpected, forming an opinion that had apparently been discussed, voted on and passed by her subconscious.

Sexy was not precisely the word she would have bestowed upon a man who, for the last twenty-four hours, had done his level best to irritate her beyond measure.

No, that wasn't quite true, she amended honestly. He was just accustomed to issuing orders and having them followed. If the man would only *ask*, she told herself for the hundredth time, there wouldn't be a problem. Instead, he was inclined to be abrupt, terse and demanding. And sexy, her inner voice reminded her....

Dear Reader:

In May of 1980 Silhouette had a goal. We wanted to bring you the best that romance had to offer— heartwarming, poignant stories that would move you time and time again.

Mission impossible? Not likely, because in 1980 and all the way through to today, we have authors with the same dream we have—writers who strive to bring you stories with a distinctive medley of charm, wit, and above all, *romance*.

And this fall we're celebrating in the Silhouette Romance line—we're having a Homecoming! In September some of your all-time favorite authors are returning to their "alma mater." Then, during October, we're honored to present authors whose books always capture the magic—some of the wonderful writers who have helped maintain the heartwarming quality the Silhouette Romance line is famous for.

Come home to Romance this fall and for always. Help celebrate the special world of Silhouette Romance.

I hope you enjoy this book and the many books to come.

Sincerely,

Tara Hughes
Senior Editor
Silhouette Books

RITA RAINVILLE

Gentle Persuasion

Published by Silhouette Books New York
America's Publisher of Contemporary Romance

To my friend, Dee
And all of the years ahead

SILHOUETTE BOOKS
300 E. 42nd St., New York, N.Y. 10017

ISBN: 0-373-08535-4

First Silhouette Books printing October 1987

America's Publisher of Contemporary Romance

Printed in the U.S.A.

Books by Rita Rainville

Silhouette Romance

RITA RAINVILLE

grew up reading truckloads of romances and replotting the endings of sad movies. She has always wanted to write the kind of romances she likes to read. She finds people endlessly interesting and that is reflected in her writing. She is happily married and lives in California with her family.

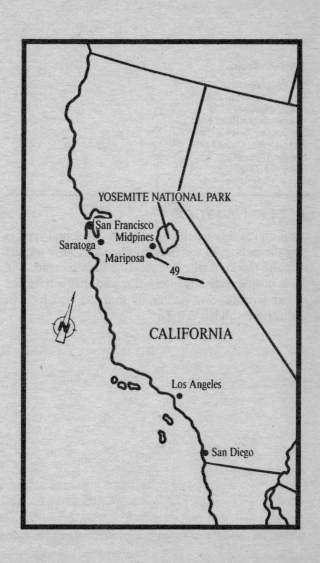

YOSEMITE NATIONAL PARK

San Francisco

Midpines

Saratoga

Mariposa

49

CALIFORNIA

Los Angeles

San Diego

Chapter One

"We've got to get rid of Edgar."

"Permanently?"

"Yes."

"How?"

"Quietly...perhaps poison."

"Suicide?"

"What do you think?"

"Probably not."

"Definitely not."

"Pity. I've grown rather fond of the old rogue."

Adam Masters slowly drew back the hand that had been poised to knock on the front porch screen door. At least that had been his intention until he heard the voices of the two women inside planning what had all the earmarks of a murder. Now he dropped his hand, waiting. If they had one functioning brain between them, he thought in resignation, they would have done their plotting behind closed doors. And he wouldn't have heard them.

If he hadn't heard them, he could have knocked on the door, introduced himself to George's sister, Opal, fulfilled his obligation to George by paying a brief visit, then left to start his vacation.

But he *had* heard them, and now he had the distinct feeling that his vacation was about to go up in smoke. Again.

"Drop in, say hello to Opal, and take a quick look around," had been his elderly partner's request. "If you pick up any strange vibes, give me a call." His tone clearly stated that while such calls were not uncommon, he hoped one wouldn't be necessary this time.

Well, Adam thought, intrigued in spite of himself, whatever Opal had been up to in the past, she might have just outdone herself. It was almost worth delaying his trip to find out. Almost, but not quite, he told himself firmly. Then, briskly, before he could hear any more about the unfortunate Edgar, he raised his hand and knocked on the wooden frame of the old-fashioned screen door.

"I'll get it." At the sound of the demanding triple rap, Kaylie West lowered her bare feet from their resting place on the round coffee table and stood up. "Are you expecting anyone?" she asked her godmother.

Opal Shriver looked up from her spiral notebook with an abstracted air. "What?"

"I said, are you expecting anyone?" Kaylie repeated patiently.

"No. Not that I know of. I don't think so."

"That wasn't a multiple-choice question," Kaylie said with a grin, padding across the rug to the door.

"Maybe it's the repairman to fix the stove," Opal said vaguely, frowning at her handwritten notes. "Although I thought he wasn't coming until next week."

He didn't look like any repairman she had ever seen, Kaylie decided, stepping out onto the screened porch and eyeing the deeply tanned, solidly built man on the top stair. But then, no one in the small California town of Saratoga seemed clearly definable. Opal's neighbor, who scrounged around in knee-high rubber boots, the one she had thought was the gardener, owned a couple of Silicon Valley's high-tech companies. The exotically dressed woman down the road was a school principal. And, God knows, Opal's little-old-gray-haired-lady routine was certainly deceptive.

"You're a week early," Kaylie informed the man, darting a quick glance at his blue knit shirt and faded jeans. His return gaze, even diffused by the screen, was a green and gold blast of male appreciation. Ah well, she decided with a startled blink, they were probably too laid-back in this neck of the woods for uniforms with company names neatly embroidered on shirt pockets. Or, for that matter, properly tethered glances. "Not that we're not delighted to see you," she assured him, pulling the screen door open and gesturing for him to enter.

"The left burners died yesterday, and we don't know how long the others will last," she explained, leading him into the kitchen. "We raised the lid and poked around, but we didn't see anything that looked unusual," she added helpfully. Her tone grew doubtful as she stood beside the stove. "The problem is, neither of us knows what things look like when they're usual."

Adam followed, wondering if she was always so casual about inviting strange men into the house. At least in this case, it had worked in his favor. No awkward explanations had been required to get him in. He slowly raised his contemplative gaze from long tan legs and a fetching derriere covered by red shorts to where his green-gold eyes met anxious blue ones.

"Do you think you can fix it?" Kaylie asked. She watched as the man silently looked at the stove, then fiddled with a couple of knobs. After a long pause, she shrugged and said, "If you need me for anything, call. I'll be in the living room."

She dropped down into the chair across from Opal. "What kind of poison?" she asked, picking up the conversational thread where she had left it.

"I don't know," the older woman said, looking up with a frown. "Something different. I can't use any of the methods I've used before."

"God forbid," Kaylie said.

Before? Adam wondered, easing up the stove lid and bracing it. An old model, he noted automatically, made well before the advent of electronic starters. One quick glance was all it took to find the problem. Wondering idly what women learned in the day-to-day process of living, he reached for the damp dishcloth folded on the sink countertop. It didn't take a mechanical genius to see that something had boiled over and sealed the opening of the pilot light. Of course, as the owner of the skimpy red shorts had said, it helps if you know what you're looking for. The something in question had probably oozed down, snuffed out the light, then hardened as the metal cooled. Using the damp cloth as a swab and the tine of a fork for a probe, he only took a few seconds to remove the rubbery stuff. Then he looked in a nearby cupboard, found a toothpick and touched it to the right-hand pilot light. He moved the burning stick over, lowered it and watched as the left pilot puffed and settled into a small blue flame. As he turned the control knobs, all four burners flared into life.

"I thought this would get easier with practice," he heard Opal comment in mild complaint, "but it seems harder all the time."

Practice? Adam's brows shot up as he lowered the top of the stove. George had obviously missed a few pertinent calls along the way.

"I was toying with the idea of castor beans," Opal said suddenly.

"What about them?" Kaylie asked in a lazy voice.

"They're highly poisonous. I thought maybe I could grind some up and add them to his salad some evening. Edgar's a vegetarian, you know."

"That all depends on how they taste," Kaylie finally said, breaking a thoughtful pause. "If they're bitter, he'll just dump the salad."

Opal scribbled a note in her book. "I'll look into that. But what do you think of the idea?"

"I can tell you one thing for sure," said a deep voice from the doorway. "George won't like it at all."

The two women turned at the sound of the gritty baritone, Opal with interest, Kaylie with resignation. It never failed. Opal drew people the same way a picnic did ants—all sorts of people with all sorts of stories to tell or opinions to express. Kaylie was convinced that if she and her godmother were stranded on an island in the middle of nowhere, a third person would swim over merely to tell Opal his most intimate secrets. Now, apparently, they were going to listen to the local repairman's thoughts on killing off Opal's latest victim.

Trying to head him off at the pass, she asked, "Is the stove fixed?"

"Why won't he?" Opal asked at the same time.

A flicker of irritation narrowed Kaylie's eyes as the tall man took his time about answering, first settling his wide shoulders more comfortably against the door-jamb. His hazel gaze inched slowly down from her mass of tawny hair to her bare feet before he acknowledged her question.

"Yes, it's fixed." He turned his head to look at Opal. "I just don't think he'll like you getting involved with poisoning people," he said carefully.

"Really?" Opal's eyes widened in surprise. "I didn't think he cared one way or another."

"How much do we owe you?" Kaylie asked, deciding that the circumstances called for assertive action. To her eternal disgust, she shifted uneasily and blinked as the full blast from those green-gold eyes was turned back on her.

"It's on the house," he said finally, his shoulders lifting in a slight shrug. "He cares," he assured Opal, watching as the older woman absorbed his words.

"Strange," she murmured. "Since he's never objected to guns or knives, I certainly don't know why he'd cavil at castor beans. It's really much neater," she pointed out hopefully. "And quieter."

Adam's eyes narrowed at her thoughtful tone. If George had never registered a complaint about the diminutive woman's strange pastime, he could understand her surprise. But his partner wasn't one to remain silent when things weren't to his liking, so obviously George didn't know. One telephone call, he decided. That was all that stood between him and a mountain vacation. One quick telephone call, and he could wash his hands of the dipsy little lady. Then, slanting a thoughtful glance at her barefoot companion, he reflected that, all things considered, it didn't pay to rush into things. After all, he could visit his cabin in the mountains anytime.

"I think I'll let George explain the finer points," he told Opal.

"How do you happen to know George?" Kaylie asked with sudden suspicion. The feeling had been growing stronger with each passing moment: the man was no ordinary repairman. Aside from the fact that he didn't look the part, his whole attitude was wrong. Any service rep with an ounce of sense would not allow his gaze to rove so appreciatively over the females he encountered in the line of business. Opal, with her usual knack for concentrating on the issue at hand—which at this moment seemed to be castor beans—had not even thought it strange that a man coming in to fix the stove would suddenly start telling her what her brother did and didn't like.

"George and I go back a long way," was his bland reply.

Kaylie's suspicions deepened as she focused her entire attention on the man in the doorway. Her blue eyes took in the length, breadth and strength of him. A man in his early thirties, she thought, or maybe just a tad older, a man much like the detective in Opal's current book. His dark, slightly long hair had a natural part and seemed to fall neatly in place with no additional help from him. It was a good thing, she decided, because he obviously wasn't the type to stand in front of a mirror with a blow-drier and a brush. A couple of swipes with a comb was probably all he would give it. And then there were his sharp hazel eyes. They didn't so much look *at* things as *through* them. Except for right now. They were examining *her* with the greatest of care, she noted.

He was a composition of strong lines. High cheek-bones, thick brows and deep brackets around a firm mouth formed a face that showed every one of his thirty-plus years. For the most part, he remained carefully poker-faced, a man, she reflected silently, who didn't give much of himself away. There was an aura of competence about him, an agile strength that would flow smoothly into action when needed. He would absorb a situation at a glance, analyze it and take whatever action was necessary, she judged. He was, in fact, the prototype of what psychologists called the alpha man: decisive, resolute, bigger than life.

Opal's scrutiny had been just as lengthy and detailed as her own, Kaylie noted, intrigued by the expression on her godmother's face. It was the look she got when she was puzzled, when—

"Adam Masters!" Opal said triumphantly.

Kaylie looked at her in surprise.

Startled, Adam inclined his head in acknowledgment.

"Who's Adam Masters?" Kaylie asked.

"He is," Opal said, pointing at the lounging man.

"But who *is* Adam Masters?" Kaylie persisted, carefully not looking in his direction.

"George's partner," Opal said, as if that should explain everything.

"How do you know?" Kaylie asked, startled. She knew for a fact that her godmother had never met the man.

Adam remained silent. He, too, was interested in how the older woman had pinpointed him so quickly.

"Just from some things George said about him," Opal said vaguely, satisfying neither of her listeners. "Besides, he doesn't have a clipboard or a tool belt."

"A clipboard?" Adam asked in spite of himself.

"Haven't you ever noticed? Repairmen usually have them," Opal explained kindly. "It's almost obligatory."

Adam sighed and briefly closed his eyes. When he opened them, he caught the amused expression on the younger woman's face.

Kaylie tried to outstare him and failed miserably. Oh, well, her talents lay in other directions, she reminded herself, not in dealing with barely polite men and barely leashed aggression.

Quiet settled over the room. Of the three of them, Opal was the most comfortable, Kaylie decided. Her godmother's expectant gaze was taking in the silent man from head to toe. It wasn't easy to read Adam Masters, but he seemed to be satisfied with the situation as it was progressing. Now his eyes turned curiously back to her.

"I'm Kaylie West," she said finally, before he could ask. "Visiting with my godmother for a while," she added, pointing to Opal.

"Ms. West," he said in polite acknowledgment, then resumed his conversation with Opal. "About the bodies?" he prompted.

"I don't know why, at this stage of the game, George is concerning himself with my affairs," she said, a frown drawing her gray brows together behind the tortoiseshell frames of her glasses.

"Exactly how long have you been, uh, disposing of people?" Adam asked in a neutral voice.

"Oh, for years!"

"Years," he repeated grimly.

"Fourteen or fifteen at least." She looked at Kaylie inquiringly. "Isn't that about right?"

Kaylie nodded, biting back a grin at the sight of Adam's scowl. Whatever George had told his partner, there were obviously some gaping holes in the story.

"It's really quite a relaxing hobby," Opal assured Adam, waving him to a chair beside her. "The difficult part is finding a foolproof method."

"Opal," Kaylie interrupted, "I think that George forgot to mention to Adam—"

"You see," Opal confided, "technology is so advanced these days, with all the lab tests they have . . ."

"That you're O. P. Shriver," Kaylie said, raising her voice.

" . . . it isn't easy to come up with—"

"What?" Adam's voice wasn't loud. It didn't have to be.

Both women stopped talking and looked at him.

"O. P. Shriver, the author?" he asked.

They nodded.

"O. P. Shriver, the noted mystery writer?" he pressed, thinking of the four paperbacks in his suitcase written by that very person.

They nodded again.

"And Edgar?"

"My latest victim," Opal said with relish.

"Yes," Adam said with massive control, leaning his head back on the chair and staring up at the ceiling. "He forgot to mention that."

After a long pause, Opal broke the silence. Turning to Adam, she asked, "How do *you* feel about castor beans?"

* * *

"Adam's going to stay with us for several days," Opal said. The two women were preparing lunch, working smoothly together in the large old kitchen.

"Here?" Kaylie asked, mentally kissing peace and serenity goodbye.

"Mm-hmm."

"How'd that happen?"

"Well, after all, he *is* George's partner," Opal said virtuously. "And he came all this way to see me just because George asked him to."

"All what way?" Kaylie interrupted.

"From San Diego."

Kaylie took three plates from the cupboard and placed them on the table. "Did he ask to stay?"

"I don't think so," Opal said cautiously after a thoughtful pause.

"Then you asked him."

"I must have," she agreed.

"Don't you remember?" Kaylie knew the question was probably useless. Opal seemed to function on about half her cylinders when she was in the midst of a book. Part of her seemed to permanently reside in her office, mingling with her current cast of characters.

"I *must* have invited him," she finally told her god-daughter. "He's staying, isn't he?"

Confronted with that obscure bit of logic, Kaylie sighed.

"And, besides, think how safe we'll feel with a man around," she said, as if solving a problem of long standing.

Kaylie set down three glasses and stared at the older woman. "What brought that up? You've never been afraid in this house. Good grief, you don't even lock the doors at night."

"Adam's such a *solid* man," Opal said finally. "I'd feel safe around him if I *were* in danger."

"Hmm," Kaylie mumbled noncommittally, wondering if Opal would feel the same if she were forty years younger and the recipient of Adam's prowling male glances. "George retired from the police department a couple of years ago, didn't he?"

Opal nodded. "Three years. He went into the security end of things, and Adam became his partner."

"The word 'security' covers a big field," Kaylie observed. "What exactly do they do?"

"Sell it. To industries and wealthy homeowners." Opal piled mounds of lunch meat on a plate.

"Since George is one of the most outspoken men I know, it's hard to picture him as a salesman. And after seeing how Adam leaps right to the point, I'm surprised they sell anything. His bedside manner leaves a lot to be desired."

"George is really the high-tech man," Opal explained. "Apparently he's added all sorts of new and devious refinements to sensors. The heat, light and noise kind," Opal said vaguely. "There seems to be no end to his ingenuity. In fact, he helped me out several times when I painted myself into corners." She waved a handful of lettuce leaves. "In my books, you know. Adam's job is to view the client's site and recommend appropriate hardware installations. I think that's where the selling comes in."

Kaylie winced as she imagined such a scene. "He's probably terrific at the evaluating part, but I bet from that point on, it's all downhill. He probably tells people what they need and expects them to believe his every word. I don't get the impression that he'd spend much time holding a client's hand or convincing them that he knows what he's talking about.''

"You may be right," Opal agreed, setting a pitcher of iced tea on the table. "George said that Adam is an ex-Green Beret and quite dynamic," she added, apropos of nothing.

"Direct, too," Kaylie muttered. "And about as tactful as a karate chop."

"So," Kaylie said to Adam later that afternoon, "I hear you're joining the household for a few days."

Over lunch, the three of them had discussed, among other things, the merits of castor beans versus other poisonous berries, shrubs and trees. Adam, she had learned during that time, was a man who took things seriously, and of all the things he regarded seriously, Security—with the appropriate capital letter—headed the list. But that was understandable, she reminded herself, trying to be forbearing. It was his business.

After they had eaten, Opal had wandered away to her office to write, leaving Kaylie to take Adam on a tour of the large old house. Her stint as tour guide hadn't given him much pleasure, she thought with a wry smile. In the short time they were together, she became aware that he frowned a lot. She had pointed out architectural points of interest; he had noted tree limbs giving easy access to the second floor. She had indicated lush bowers, furnished with white wrought-iron furniture and bright, fat cushions; he had mentioned hiding places for intruders.

Now he leaned back in a wicker chair, examining the wood-framed screen door with narrowed eyes, and Kaylie made a mental wager that he was already picturing stout locks on every door.

"Anyone with a knife or a credit card could flip the latch on that door," he informed her.

I win, Kaylie thought with an inward smile of satisfaction. "They wouldn't have to," she said. "It's never locked."

"Do you always just open the door and let people in?" Adam asked, turning to her with genuine curiosity.

"I wouldn't at home," she acknowledged, thinking briefly of the doorman posted in the lobby of her San Francisco apartment building. "But out here it's different." She determinedly refused to think of what had happened the day before and waved a hand to indicate the surrounding area. "Once you get off the main drag, you're in the country."

He inclined his head politely. "And burglars don't live in the country?"

Kaylie contemplated his expressionless face with a resigned look. "I suppose they do," she admitted finally, knowing she couldn't divert him from the coming lecture. He had a point to make, and, come hell or high water, he was going to get it out of his system. "But I think most of them stay in the cities, where they can empty out stores. Besides, I don't think they'd come knocking on the door the way you did."

"You didn't ask to see my ID," he pointed out evenly. "You didn't even ask if I was a repairman. You just threw open the door and led me into the kitchen."

"Don't you think you're just a wee bit paranoid on the subject?" She got up and padded over to the door, where she stared dreamily out at the lush summer foliage. "I think your line of work tends to tilt your thinking—and skew your trust mechanism. I couldn't live like that, suspecting everyone.'' In spite of yesterday. ''Most people are really nice, you know.''

A muttered word emerged deep from Adam's throat. ''Perhaps.'' His tone indicated that he was striving for politeness, but he was lying through his teeth. ''Do you have any idea how many outside doors this place has on the first floor alone?'' he asked.

''Five,'' she replied promptly. ''Do I get a gold star?''

''And how many do you suppose are locked at night, or when you're both gone?'' he persisted.

''All of them?'' she asked, giving wide-eyed innocence her best shot. The fact that it didn't work came as no surprise.

''Hardly. One lock is so rusty it's shedding, and another is frozen. When I turned the key, it broke.''

''Two good reasons for not locking them, I'd say.''

Her vivid face, alight with amusement, almost distracted him. Almost. With a sigh, he dragged his mind back to the business at hand. Around Kaylie West, he was discovering, that was no easy task. ''Maybe. But there's no excuse for not replacing them.''

''How are the other three?''

''If you bother to lock them—'' his emphasis on the first word expressed his doubt ''—a first-grader could open them.''

Kaylie tried to match his concern. Opal wasn't a fool. Nor was she unaware of the criminal element loose in the world. In doing her meticulous research, she spent a considerable amount of time with law enforcers in their natural habitat. She didn't seem to feel personally threatened by what she had seen, and if she wanted to sleep with her windows open and her door locks frozen, then that was the way it would be.

She would make one more attempt to divert the man beside her, Kaylie decided, although heaven only knew why. She probably wouldn't budge his one-track mind—and he was a lot more dangerous when he wasn't thinking about business, anyway. However, she decided nobly, for his own good, she'd give it a try.

"If you forget the first-graders who have to be in before dark, who's around here to break in?" Her hands lifted in a gesture that took in the quiet, tree-lined street and the rural atmosphere of the entire area. "There's not a person to be seen, and the only sounds are birds singing and a few leaves rattling in the breeze. It's not exactly a criminal's paradise." One incident did not a high-crime area make, she reminded herself.

Adam sighed again and watched as she brushed a strand of hair back, patting it in place. It promptly fell over her brow. In one short afternoon he had become addicted to watching her hair. Its shimmering mass reminded him of the color of autumn leaves and was one of the reasons he was sitting on the porch of this old house instead of heading for the Sierras. The other reasons were dark blue eyes that smiled, a face that wasn't beautiful but was animated with intelligence and humor, a generous mouth, and a sweet, sassy bottom.

He had the distinct feeling that Opal's preoccupation with her current book was responsible for his easy access into the house. He hadn't asked to stay. He had been thinking of a tactful approach—not his strongest suit—when the conversation with the older woman had become incredibly convoluted. Kaylie hadn't been in the room at the time. He had been in the midst of trying to untangle the verbal exchange when she'd returned. He'd stopped abruptly when he realized that somewhere along the way Opal had said he could have the upstairs bedroom that overlooked the backyard.

Tact might not be one of his sterling qualities, he reflected wryly, but he knew how to make the most of what he had. And what he had was propinquity.

He intended to use it.

Chapter Two

W ho would break in here?'' Kaylie repeated the question, wondering what had brought about the resolute expression on Adam's face.

"Almost anyone who wanted to make a fast buck," he said absently. "The real question, though, is how easy would it be to get in? Come with me for a minute," he said, getting to his feet and holding out his hand to her. "I want to show you a few things."

His extended hand wrapped around her wrist, and he opened the door with the other one. As they walked around to the back of the house, Adam looked down at the woman beside him. He was having a hard time doing anything *but* looking at her, he acknowledged wryly. Kaylie was a bit taller than average, the top of her head hitting just a little above his chin. Her hair was unconfined and fell around her face and shoulders in sexy abandon. His choice of words surprised him, slowing his thoughts down for a second, and he tried them again. Sexy abandon. Yes, he decided, that was a fair description. Of course, she probably thought it was simply a casual hair style. But any man would take one look and know it for what it was.

The rest of her was just as fascinating, he decided, examining a face that reflected her every emotion. Her eyes were set far apart beneath thick, shapely brows and were framed by extravagant lashes. Her mouth was wide and sweet and vulnerable. He would definitely taste those lips before he left for the mountains, he promised himself. If he left for the mountains.

"Opal likes the natural look," she explained, pulling him to a stop and waving a hand at small paths that wound through ancient oaks, meandered under archways of ivy and wandered past massive rhododendrons.

"Charming," Adam muttered, his gaze swinging to the house.

Kaylie stared in surprise. "You don't like it?"

"It's fine. I just wish she had spent as much time and energy on the house. Other than paint and general upkeep, nothing's been done to this place in years."

"It looks fine to me," she said loyally, glaring up at him.

Pointing at the sparkling windows, he said, "I bet not one out of ten has a working lock. And look at that oak tree." He indicated the one that had caught his attention earlier. "Anyone could climb that branch right up to the bedroom window."

"If you're going to suggest cutting it off, forget it," she said flatly. "Whoever said that hell has no fury like a woman scorned hadn't seen Opal protecting her trees. It's so bad that when the gardener comes to prune, he prays that she's out of town."

"Has George seen this place?" he demanded.

"Not in years. Opal keeps him away."

He swore softly. "Well, I'm at least going to take care of the doors and windows."

Kaylie's widened eyes never left his face. She examined him with the same fascination that a scientist might use when scrutinizing a creature from outer space. "Let me get this straight," she said slowly. "You're going to bore holes in these gorgeous old wooden doors and install great big locks without even asking Opal?"

"I owe it to George."

And what about Opal? Kaylie wondered. Doesn't it matter what she wants?

"How's it coming?"

"Not too bad."

It was early the next afternoon, and Kaylie stood in the doorway of one of the upstairs bedrooms. She held a can of beer in one hand and a large glass of iced tea in the other, watching as Adam carefully chiseled away layers of old paint from the window frame.

He was obviously a morning person. Before she had wandered into the kitchen looking for her first cup of coffee, he had returned from the hardware store with a box. She'd found him sitting at the table with Opal, explaining that he was going to replace the broken locks on her windows. Opal had nodded absently, picked up her notebook and headed for her office.

"That sounded like the opening salvo," Kaylie had commented.

"How's that?" Adam lifted his cup and stared at her over its rim.

"First the windows, then the doors. Then come the dead bolts and chains. Somewhere down the road are windows wired for sound and an alarm panel by the door. Where does it all end?''

Adam shrugged. ''When the house is as safe as it should be.''

''Opal thinks it's fine as it is,'' Kaylie said.

''I think she's too preoccupied to give it any thought at all,'' Adam pointed out. ''To my way of thinking, the people who care about her should attend to it. The same way they'd fix a loose board on the front steps.''

''That's an entirely different matter!''

He shook his head and said mildly, ''No, it isn't. We're talking about prevention. It's all the same thing.''

''You're going to make this place into a prison,'' Kaylie grumbled, turning away with her coffee and leaving the room.

She had spent the morning in a frenzy of cleaning, working off her bad temper. The problem, she decided, was that Adam hadn't spent his childhood summers with Opal. He had no idea of the freedom this house represented. Or what memories she had of running up the front stairs and always finding the doors open, as if the house was greeting her with outstretched arms. Now, cooled off and determined not to lose her temper again, she stood with her peace offering.

The other problem he had, she reflected, noting with interest how his knit shirt clung to his broad-shouldered frame, was that he had worked with men for too long. He didn't know the first thing about building a relationship with a woman. A working relationship, she clarified silently. Heaven alone knew how he handled the more personal side of his life. Watching his biceps swell as he applied pressure to lift the stubborn lock, she told herself that she had no interest in the subject. None at all. Not an iota. Not even a jot.

"Shouldn't take too long to do these," Adam said, glancing down at the remaining contents of the box. "Most of them are just held on by paint." He eyed the sweating aluminum can with anticipation. "Is that for me?" Taking it from her outstretched hand, he lifted it in a brief toast and downed half the can. "Thanks, honey. That hit the spot."

Honey. Somehow, in the brief span of twenty-four hours, she'd gone from Ms. West to Kaylie to, occasionally, honey. And, for some reason, she didn't mind. Possibly because, coming from Adam Masters, the words had a natural, rather absentmindedly affectionate sound. At least they did when she wasn't furious with him. And after the past few years of holding her own in the business world, a little affection was unexpectedly disarming.

"Only a few more to go," he said, pressing down on the screwdriver with easy strength.

"Tennessee!" she said with the deep satisfaction of one who had finally solved a knotty problem.

"Tennessee, what?" He fitted in the last screw, his back to her.

"You were born in Tennessee, went to school for a few years in the Southwest, probably Oklahoma, then moved to the West Coast. Right?"

He turned, puzzled, looking at her as if he had caught her stirring a caldron of newt's eyes. "Right. How'd you know?" he asked finally.

"It's just a hobby," she said with a slight smile. "Sorry if I startled you, but you were a tough nut to crack. It took me longer than it usually does. You've come a long way from your Southern roots."

"I left when I was eight and I've never been back," he said absently, thinking that she didn't look apologetic. She looked quite pleased with herself, as a matter of fact. With reason, he acknowledged, having firmly believed that he had lost all traces of his origin. "But that doesn't answer my question." He tucked the screwdriver in the back pocket of his jeans and propped one shoulder against the wall.

"I worked my way through college typing notes for Professor Wyckoff, a phonetician." She dropped down on the foot of the bed, folding one leg beneath her.

Adam waited politely.

"He was writing a book on regional accents," she added, as if that explained everything. One look at Adam's expression told her it didn't. "I worked for him for four years. When he saw that I was actually interested in his project, not just typing words, he stopped scribbling notes and had me work directly from tapes. I listened to a zillion of them, accents from all over the country." She smiled, remembering the old man's enthusiasm. "Business was my major, but I spent a lot of time in his lab and absorbed things like a sponge."

"A useful talent," Adam commented, turning back to the window.

Shrugging dismissively, Kaylie said, "Not really. I liven up a party every now and then, but it's not much more than a parlor trick." She took a swallow of tea. "Sometimes it helped me build rapport with a client."

She turned her head, following his progress, taking in his lithe grace. His large, well-shaped hands moved absently over the window frame, stopping at the center rail to test the lock. When it jiggled, he reached for the screwdriver in his pocket, his fingers closing around the fluted amber handle. Seconds later he was absorbed in removing the screws.

He makes that look so simple, she thought with envy. Screwdrivers, she knew from experience, were not that easy to control. They had a nasty habit of sliding out of the slotted screw heads, then skittering around and gouging the surrounding surface. They got up to all sorts of mishaps unless sternly supervised.

There was something decidedly sexy about competence, she reflected idly.

For one short, awful moment Kaylie thought she had said the words aloud. They were totally unexpected, forming an opinion that had apparently been discussed, voted on and passed by her subconscious. *Sexy* was not precisely the word she would have bestowed upon a man who, for the past twenty-four hours, had done his level best to irritate her beyond measure. No, that wasn't quite true, she amended honestly. To give credit where it was due, he didn't have to work at it; it was something that came naturally. She had learned one thing in that short time: he was accustomed to issuing orders and having them followed. She, unfortunately, was not a person who enjoyed being on the receiving end of such orders.

She'd held her breath the night before, anticipating Opal's negative response when he had calmly informed the older woman that he intended to beef up the security level of the house. She had been disappointed. Opal had looked up from a book on poisonous shrubs and said vaguely that she didn't care what he did as long as he was quiet and didn't disturb her while she was writing. After a moment's thought, she'd added that she didn't like to carry a lot of keys, then returned to her book.

What was most annoying, Kaylie admitted to herself, was the fact that she was intrigued by him. He had a dry sense of humor that surfaced when she least expected it, completely disarming her. And she had no logical reason to resent what he was doing. As a matter of fact, when she was on her own turf she was almost as paranoid about locks as he was. So what was her problem? *He* was. She found his assumption that she would do whatever he directed her to do quite maddening. As a result, when he told her that she *would* lock the doors and *wouldn't* leave the house until she poked certain buttons in the soon-to-be-installed control panel, she'd turned quite illogical and contrary. If the man would only *ask*, she told herself for the hundredth time, there wouldn't be a problem. Instead, he was inclined to be abrupt, terse and demanding. And sexy, her inner voice reminded her.

"Rapport with what kind of client?" Adam asked. "What do you do?"

"Real estate," she said succinctly. "Past tense, not present. I called it quits last month."

He tore another lock out of its plastic envelope and set it on the rail. "Why?"

Kaylie rose and tilted her glass in a see-you-later gesture. "I got tired of fighting the sharks and piranhas."

Adam watched her go out the door and turn into the hall. Since meeting her, he had developed a morbid fascination with cataloging their differences. She was impulsive, with a frisky sense of humor lurking in her blue eyes, waiting to dart out at the slightest provocation. Her hair, that mass of golden-brown stuff that swung so tantalizingly with her every step, seemed to shimmer with energy. In fact, he decided, moving to the next window, if you discounted sweetly flaring hips and breasts that would nicely fill a man's hands—his hands—she was a bit like a puppy, charging into life, eyes bright with expectancy.

The problem was, he was neither trusting nor credulous. In contrast, he felt like a suspicious, bad-tempered Great Dane. More times than he cared to count, he had watched her expression change from warmth to cool formality as a result of something he'd said. He was beginning to feel as if he had a permanent case of foot-in-mouth disease. What it all boiled down to was that he didn't know how to deal with women. There had, of course, been women in his life, but never a woman. A special woman.

Men, aside from the obvious dissimilarities, were different, he mused. They understood if you were terse or a bit abrupt. Men had a tendency toward succinctness. They appreciated not having to wallow through long explanations and great gobs of descriptive detail. For the most part, they just wanted the facts. To be told—briefly—what to do and how to do it.

Women, on the other hand, had all sorts of nooks and crannies in their thinking process. Just as you thought you had them settled down to consider the subject at hand, they darted down some mental alleyway and dragged back a totally irrelevant bone of contention. Then they launched into a full-fledged discussion, bearing down heavily on the extraneous issues. It was, mercifully, something which he had heretofore been spared. It was also, he decided, something he'd better get a handle on—at least, if he intended to spend much time around Kaylie. And that decision had already been made.

Later he went downstairs to the pantry, part of which was serving temporarily as his storage area. Now that the basics were done, with all the old locks on both windows and doors replaced, he could start installing the sensors. He'd opted for a hardwired system; it was less obtrusive and more reliable, since each sensor was attached directly to the control panel.

Scowling, he recalled his conversation with Kaylie about the panel. She was going to give him a hard time about it. Was? She'd already started. Her parting shot had been that she didn't want to live in a prison. Before he'd had time to remind her that it wasn't her house, she'd added that Opal wouldn't like it, either.

"Prison!" he grumbled, his disgusted tone making the word sound like an oath. Didn't the woman, for Pete's sake, understand a *shunt*? The bypass feature was designed precisely to keep people from feeling like captives in their own house. It allowed the system to remain on without having every door and window locked tight. He'd have to explain it to her. Again. And remain calm, he promised himself.

The telephone rang, and he reached out and snagged it. "Shriver residence," he said. As he listened, his eyes narrowed. He asked several brief questions and didn't like the answers. Slowly, he replaced the receiver in its cradle on the wall.

Kaylie peeked through the kitchen door, her gaze settling on Adam's back. He had the look of a man who had just received some unwelcome news, she thought. "Did I hear the phone?"

His eyes were like chips of emerald, almost as cold as his voice. "Why didn't you tell me you were involved in a store robbery?"

With an obstinate expression on her face, Kaylie came into the room. "Because it's over and done with," she told him. "It happened the day before yesterday, before you arrived. And I knew if I said anything about it, you'd turn it into a capital offense.''

"Tell me about it."

"There's nothing to tell," she said defensively. "The store was robbed; the men got away and the police came. That's it."

"Everything, Kaylie," he said softly, obviously containing himself. "I want to hear it all."

"But—"

"*Now*, Kaylie."

And that, Kaylie thought, was apparently that. He wanted to hear and expected to be told. She dropped down into one of the straight-backed chairs and glared at him.

He pulled out one for himself and sat back with grim anticipation.

For the first time she allowed herself to think back, to take the event out of the dark hole into which she had shoved it.

It had all started, she remembered, when Opal's watch had died. She had offered to take it into the jewelry store to be repaired and planned to spend some time browsing through the local shops. She had been contented and unsuspecting—in short, a perfect victim.

"Mr. Jensen?" Her question had broken into the hush of the almost empty store. The large room was long and narrow, with tasteful displays of gleaming gold and glittering diamonds. A young couple sat in an alcove looking at the engagement rings a salesman was showing them, and, near the rear, an elderly woman in black considered several strands of creamy pearls.

The slight man with a jeweler's loupe hanging from a cord around his neck looked up. He ran a hand through thinning gray hair, his abstracted gaze finally coming to rest on Kaylie's face. "Yes?"

He was a colorless little man, she reflected. With a pale face and weary eyes. He might be Opal's contemporary, but he looked much older.

"I'm Kaylie West," she told him with a smile, resting her bag on the glass counter and rummaging through it. "My godmother, Opal Shriver, asked me to bring in her watch. She's hoping that you can fix it while I wait."

"How is Opal?" he asked pleasantly, holding out his hand. A fine tremor shook it, and he abruptly dropped it to the counter and laced the fingers of both hands together.

"Fine." Her eyes darkened with warmth, silently empathizing with a man whose livelihood depended on the steadiness of his hands. "For being in the middle of a book, that is. She's holed up in her office and only comes out to eat." She removed her wallet and peered into the dark interior of her bag, muttering, "Sorry, I know it's in here somewhere."

After depositing her keys beside her wallet, she pulled out a packet of tissue, a roll of film and a folded map before she tried again. "Ah! Here it is." She withdrew the gold watch and handed it to him.

He opened the back with a deft movement. After peering inside, he looked up with a slight movement of his lips that seemed to serve for a smile. "The battery," he said with resignation. "There was a time when jewelers were craftsmen. Now we replace batteries."

Kaylie nodded commiseratingly, watching as his fingers moved, gently exploring the watch.

"As long as I have it," he said with a slight frown, "I'd like to clean it and polish the bracelet. Could you leave it with me until tomorrow?"

She shook her head regretfully. "I don't think I should. I promised Opal I'd bring it back with me, and I hate to do anything that might upset her while she's working on a book. Maybe you could just put in the battery, and I'll tell her to come back when she has more time."

The jeweler looked at his own watch, then stared thoughtfully down at Opal's. "What if I do it now?"

Kaylie nodded again, appreciating the old man's persistence. He obviously valued his customers and believed in giving them his best. In a world composed of fast-food restaurants and discount stores, such service was almost a lost art. She certainly wasn't going to discourage him. "That's fine. I'm in no hurry."

The glance he shot her seemed to hold equal parts exasperation and resignation. It was obvious that he didn't want her hovering at his elbow. "It may take a while. If you have other things to do, errands to run or shopping, you might prefer to come back in a couple of hours," he suggested quietly.

An hour later Kaylie swung back through the door. It appeared to be lunchtime, because the salesman was gone. The jeweler and the old woman shopping for pearls were the only occupants. She was early, but Mr. Jensen would just have to put up with her.

"Hi, Mr. Jensen." She raised her hand and fluttered her fingers in a here-I-am-again gesture.

He looked away from the old lady, who was still scrutinizing the pearls. "I'll be right with you."

"No hurry," she said politely, moving a discreet distance away to eye a sapphire and diamond ring.

Then, with no warning at all, terror entered the elegant showroom.

"Everyone down on the floor," a man's sharp voice said behind her.

Kaylie whirled and stared up into a face misshapen by a woman's sheer stocking.

"I said *down on the floor.*"

Kaylie's knees locked, and she stood frozen in disbelief as a second man shut the door, turned the Closed sign to the street and then walked over to stand beside his accomplice. Kaylie's stomach churned with nausea as she looked at the distorted features of the two men.

"Lady, don't make him tell you again." The surprising softness of the voice added to the upheaval in her stomach. She dropped quickly to her knees, and then fell flat on the floor. She noted that Mr. Jensen was sinking behind the glass counter with his hands raised, and the old woman had crumpled, becoming a black pool on the garnet rug.

"You, Mr. Jeweler, keep your hands up and come here," the first man ordered, moving forward and planting his feet by Kaylie's face.

Startled by the movement, Kaylie opened her eyes and stared straight at a scruffy deck shoe. Originally dark blue, it now had a grayish sheen and was mottled with spots. Above that was a skinny, pale, bare ankle, stained with red.

Closing her eyes, she slowly buried her nose in the thick plush carpet. Not one heroic thought crossed her mind. She didn't try to talk the men into leaving. She didn't grab the skinny ankle and attempt to bring the man down. She didn't do anything except grind her nose into the rug, listen to the men order poor Mr. Jensen to empty the display cases, hope that the poor old lady hadn't gone into cardiac arrest, and pray that the gun wouldn't go off.

"That's right, buddy, the next case," the sharp voice commanded. *"Move it!"*

"Easy now, Billy, don't rattle the man."

"Rattle, hell. He's stalling."

"I think he's moving as quick as his old bones will let him," the softer voice disagreed. "Old man, the faster you move, the safer you'll be," he advised mildly.

Feet moved near Kaylie's head, and she tried to make herself smaller.

"Those, buddy, put 'em in this bag." Something heavy rapped the glass counter. *"Those,* I said. The diamonds. All of them!"

"Don't break the case, Billy," the calm voice directed. "There might be a shock sensor on it."

The muscles in Kaylie's back tightened as silence fell. It was broken only by the clink of jewelry dropping into a bag, harsh breathing above her and a slight asthmatic wheeze from behind the glass case.

"That's right, the tray of rings."

"I'll see to the phones," the second man said.

"Hurry. That's really good," the sharp voice mocked. "Keep it up."

"Okay." The soft-voiced man returned. "Ready?"

"Almost."

A foot nudged Kaylie's hip. A convulsive shudder tore through her body, and her fingers dug into the deep pile of the rug.

"Don't be in a hurry to open the door after we leave," came the quiet command. "Hear me?"

Kaylie nodded without opening her eyes and shuddered again as a soft laugh drifted down.

The door opened and closed. The quality of the silence told Kaylie all she needed to know. Terror and the two men were gone.

Her muscles suddenly slack, Kaylie lifted heavy lids and looked up at Mr. Jensen. Moving stiffly, he turned, stabbed at a button concealed in a carved wooden panel, then moved around in front of the glass case. His knees buckled, and he slowly slid to the floor.

"Dear, merciful God," he muttered. "We're still alive."

"Kaylie? *Kaylie?* Hey, don't fade away on me—at least, not until you've told me about the robbery." Adam stared in concern at her still, solemn face, then calmly picked her up and sat down, settling her across his thighs. Before she could stir, Opal came through the swinging door into the kitchen.

She stopped, blinking at the two of them from behind her tortoiseshell frames. "Ah, Kaylie. Did you have a chance to call the nursery and ask Mr. Tanaka about the oleander bushes?"

Kaylie dug her elbow into Adam's ribs, but his arm just gathered her closer, until she was pressed against his chest. "Sorry," she wheezed. "Not yet."

Opal dropped down into Kaylie's empty chair, staring at them with unseeing eyes. "Edgar is turning into a problem," she said morosely. "I knew he was going to give me trouble the minute he came down in that hot-air balloon."

"What's he doing?" Adam asked blankly.

"It's what he *isn't* doing that's driving me nuts."

Slanting her a faintly amused glance, he tried again. "What isn't he doing?"

She glared at him, thoroughly disgusted. "He won't eat the castor beans."

"Won't?" he asked in understandable confusion. "Can't you make him?"

She blinked her smoky eyes, taken off guard for a moment. "Well, of course. Eventually. But sometimes it's...difficult." Her gaze shifted to Kaylie. "He said they looked like chopped olives on his salad, and he hates black olives. He dumped it in the sink. The salad," she clarified.

Kaylie tugged at Adam's hand, but couldn't budge it. "You didn't know he, uh, had an aversion to olives?" she ventured.

"I never thought about it, and that annoys me, too." She grew thoughtful as she considered the situation. "I just may have to give up on the castor beans. That's why I need to know about the oleanders."

She made a move to get up, then suddenly decided to stay where she was. "Kaylie, why are you sitting in Adam's lap?"

Chapter Three

"She's going to tell me a story." Adam's arm remained firmly around Kaylie's waist.

Kaylie looked at Opal's expectant expression. "But she isn't going to open her mouth until she gets a chair of her own."

After a pause that lasted long enough to make Kaylie distinctly nervous, Adam released her—or, at least, most of her. His hand remained wrapped around her wrist until she settled into the chair next to his. Ignoring the irritation narrowing her blue eyes, he prompted, "The robbery."

Opal blinked. "Robbery?"

"I told you about it." Kaylie looked across the table at the other woman. "Remember? Mr. Jensen's jewelry store?"

Opal's gray curls tossed as she shook her head vigorously. "You couldn't have. I'm sure I wouldn't forget a thing like that. Would I?" she added in sudden doubt.

"If I remember correctly," Kaylie said with a wry smile, "you told me it was very interesting and asked if I knew anything about poisons."

Adam, cutting through Opal's apology, said firmly, "We're listening now." Then, before Kaylie could draw a breath, he asked, "Were you hurt?" His gaze ran over her, seeming to take inventory.

Kaylie blinked in surprise as something cold and dangerous coiled in his eyes. She shook her head. "No. They just scared the life out of me."

"Was anybody hurt?" Opal inquired.

"No, thank God. There were just three of us—Mr. Jensen, an old lady and me—in the store when they came in."

Adam covered her tightly folded hands with his. "Your fingers are cold." When he was satisfied that she was warming up nicely, he said evenly, "I want to know everything that happened."

Opal walked over to the stove and poured three mugs of coffee. Placing them on the round oak table, she motioned for Kaylie and Adam to move their chairs closer.

Kaylie took a long swallow of the streaming brew. "It was almost eleven when I took Opal's watch in to Mr. Jensen," she said obediently.

"Is that when it happened?" Adam asked, his face taut with concentration.

Surprised, she shook her head. "No. I left it with him and I went shopping. I was gone for about an hour."

Adam sighed. He had asked for everything, and, if he wasn't careful, he'd get a blow-by-blow description of each store she had visited. If he had said the same thing to a man, he reflected wryly, by now he'd be listening to the details of the holdup. "Everything about the robbery," he prompted with studied patience.

"I was looking at some rings when two men walked in." Kaylie spoke deliberately, trying to remain objective. But even in the security of the warm kitchen, she shivered as she told them of that last, soft laugh before the two men went out the door. Finally she looked up from her coffee mug, where her finger was tracing a monotonous path around its rim. Lingering traces of disquiet clouded her eyes as her gaze met Adam's. "Then Mr. Jensen punched the alarm button," she concluded with a shrug. "We spent the rest of the time reviving Mrs. Grimaldi, the little old lady in black," she explained. "And that's what we were doing when the police arrived."

Adam lifted his mug and swallowed deeply. "And what did they have to say?"

"Say? Nothing." Kaylie sighed. "But they never ran out of questions. They wanted to know what the men looked like, what—"

"What *did* they look like?" Adam and Opal asked at the same time.

"Like most of the men walking around on the street—average height, average weight. They wore jeans, knit shirts and scruffy sneakers. And their faces—" she remembered them with a wince "—were all distorted from the stockings." She was suddenly grateful that she wasn't prone to nightmares. If she had been, those faces and that soft, menacing laugh would have supplied the perfect material, she reflected.

"Wasn't there anything special about them?" Opal asked in disappointment.

Kaylie's lips curved up in a half smile. Now that the story was over, and Opal knew that everyone had survived intact, she was allowing her professional curiosity to take over. "I didn't have much time to look them over," she said in mock apology. "If you remember, I was told to get down on the floor and stay there."

"How dull," Opal said disapprovingly. "You'd have to do better than that for a book. They'd need a scar or a tattoo or something. It never fails to amaze me how extraordinarily ordinary life can be."

Kaylie turned slowly to face her godmother. "What did you say?"

Some of Adam's tension had dissipated at her wry response to her godmother. Now he tensed at Kaylie's colorless little question. He could literally smell trouble.

"I said," Opal repeated placidly, "how extraordinarily or—"

"No, before that." Her eyes widened with sudden memory. "My God," she said, appalled. "That wasn't a stain—it was a tattoo!"

Opal's smoky eyes gleamed with gratification. "I knew it! What kind?"

"A jagged red thunderbolt about two inches long."

"Where was it?"

"On the inside of his right ankle."

"How did you manage to spot it there?" Adam asked grimly.

Kaylie looked at him, shrugging. "It wasn't hard. My nose was buried in the rug right by his foot." Leaning back in the chair, she groaned. "How could I miss something as obvious as that? I'm going to have to call and let the police know," she said with resignation.

"They already think I'm not playing with a full deck. Now they'll know for sure."

"It's common to forget things in a stressful situation," Opal soothed. "I'm sure they expect it."

"What are you looking for?" Adam asked, as Kaylie's gaze traveled around the kitchen.

"My bag. One of the officers gave me a business card with a case number written on it. He said I should call if anything else occurred to me."

"See?" Opal said as Adam retrieved the purse from the chair next to him. "They're used to it. They wouldn't have the cards if they weren't."

"Maybe so," Kaylie muttered, emptying the tote bag on the kitchen table, "but I'm not. It would be one thing if it was some insignificant detail, but a bright red tattoo? I feel like a fool." She pounced on a small card. "Here it is." After brooding over it for a moment, she let out a long sigh. "Well, I suppose I might as well get it over with."

"Want me to make the call?" Adam held out his hand for the card.

Kaylie shook her head. "Thanks, but I'd better do it. They'd just want to know who you are, why I'm not calling, and who knows what else. It would probably end up taking twice as long."

Adam leaned back in his chair and reached for his mug. His narrowed eyes followed her as she moved over to the telephone. A familiar rush of adrenaline surged through his body as he thought about her brush with danger. She had been damned lucky to get off as easily as she had. He had experienced enough senseless brutality in his life to know just *how* fortunate. The two men, jumpy and armed, had been a perfect invitation to disaster. Something as innocent as a knock on the door could have set them off, and instead of Kaylie driving home, there would have been a visit from the police telling Opal that she was in the hospital. Or worse.

Shaking his head, he tried to dispel the grim images. It hadn't happened. She was safe, and the whole thing was over. She couldn't identify the two punks, so she was out of the picture. And that suited him just fine. He'd seen too many things go wrong for well-intentioned citizens who tried to be helpful.

His mood of quiet satisfaction came to an abrupt end as Kaylie's voice changed. She was still speaking into the mouthpiece of the telephone, but now her words were slower and edged with impatience.

"Of course I'm sure. Otherwise I wouldn't have told the patrolman. Absolutely." Her sigh was neither subtle nor quiet. It was clearly a plea for patience. "If you think it's necessary. All right. Tomorrow morning."

Adam set down his mug and moved over to her side. Braced for bad news, he asked, "What was that all about?"

"Nothing important," she said vaguely, carefully avoiding his glance. She had been aware of his displeasure, controlled but quite evident, as she had moved away from the table. The man was totally unreasonable, she decided. The way he was acting, you'd think she had deliberately chosen to become involved in the robbery. One way or another, she reflected, her next bit of news was guaranteed to do nothing but fan the flames. Why did life have to be so difficult? she wondered morosely. After the experience she'd had, she could have done with a bit of cosseting, but she was pretty sure that she wouldn't get any of that from the large, controlled man beside her.

"Kaylie." The quiet word was a warning. It told her that he wanted an answer; he wanted it now; and he wouldn't be ignored.

"It's all so stupid," she said in a goaded voice.

He raised a hand and placed the palm on the wall just behind her shoulder, cutting off an avenue of retreat. The movement was one of deliberate intimidation. "I thought you couldn't identify them. But just now, it sounded like you were saying you could."

"I *can't*." Taking advantage of the one opening he had left, she swung to the sink at her left, filled a glass with water and downed half of it. "At least, not by their looks," she amended meticulously. Carefully setting the glass on the counter, she stood with her back to him, gazing moodily out the window.

Adam stared at her in sudden comprehension. "Oh, no, you didn't tell them that you could—"

She turned to face him, interrupting the astounded query. "Of course I did. What did you want me to do? Lie? I told the police the truth. If they ever catch the men, I can identify their voices."

"Damn it, woman, don't you have an ounce of self-preservation?"

Kaylie winced at the muted roar. "Now, Adam," she soothed, backing up as far as she could go. Unfortunately, it was no more than a couple of inches before the sink stopped her cold.

"Don't 'now, Adam' me," he bit off, towering over her. "Do you have any idea of the sorts of things that can happen to witnesses?"

Throwing up her hands in exasperation, she said defensively, "What was I supposed to do? Say I couldn't when I could? Believe me, if I can help get those two creeps off the street, I will. Besides, they were so easy to pinpoint, it was almost pathetic.''

"Easy?'' He scowled down at her, unimpressed.

"Piece of cake,'' she announced with a tentative smile. "They spent a lot of years being good ole boys down in Texas. Of course,'' she said thoughtfully, "they've smoothed off the rough edges of their accents by living in California for quite some time. By now, they probably think they sound like everyone else.''

Muttering in disgust, Adam turned to Opal. "You talk to her. Maybe you can drill some sense into her.''

Opal beamed a smile of approval at her goddaughter. "You did exactly what I would expect you to do.'' Looking up at Adam, she added briskly, "The world would be in an awful mess if we all ignored our civic responsibility.''

He walked over to the window and stared out at the late-afternoon sun, the set of his shoulders a clear indication of his disagreement. Without turning, he said, "A good-citizenship award doesn't make you bullet-proof. What if those two punks get wind of this? Kaylie would be a sitting duck.''

Kaylie thought longingly of the walk she had intended to take before she had been distracted by the telephone. She would go as soon as the interrogation was over, she vowed. She'd cut through the backyard and take the private road that curved up the hill, and she wouldn't have to answer any of Adam's questions for at least an hour. Absorbed in the delights of that agenda, she murmured absently, "How would they find out?''

"The papers, for starters.''

Opal set her mug on the table. "No, I don't think so,'' she said in a thoughtful voice. "It happened two days ago, Adam. If it hasn't appeared in the paper by now, I doubt if it will."

"Is it a large jewelry store?" He turned from the window and looked at the two women.

"Yes." They both spoke at once.

Adam retrieved his mug and refilled it. "I can't believe that every reporter in the area missed the police report."

"There was a small article yesterday morning in the San Jose paper, just a brief factual account," Kaylie told him. "It didn't even mention Mrs. Grimaldi or me by name."

"Is there a paper here in town?"

Opal nodded with obvious reluctance. "A new one is just getting off the ground."

"How often does it come out?"

"Twice a week."

"And when," he asked gently, "is the next edition?"

"Tomorrow," Kaylie said with stark simplicity. Then, with a stubbornness born of desperation, she said, "I don't believe the police would be stupid enough to tell them about a possible witness, so how would they find out?"

Adam propped one hip on the table and stared down at her, taking in her rebellious expression. "That depends on how many people were around when you explained, doesn't it?"

Kaylie groaned silently, sensing that another lecture was looming on the horizon, and that her walk was slipping farther away.

"How many were there, Kaylie?" he prodded. "Mr. Jensen?"

"Yes," she said cautiously. "But I don't think he heard. He was either busy with the patrolmen or the old lady."

"And Mrs. what's-her-name? Grimaldi?"

"A bit hazy, but she was there," she admitted.

"Did the police believe you right away, or did you have to convince them?" he asked casually.

Leaping on the change of subject with relief, she remembered her earlier frustration and scowled. "No, they didn't. When I tried to explain, they acted like I was some kind of a nut. The patrolman wouldn't even listen to me until I told him that he grew up in Indiana. That got his attention," she recalled with satisfaction. "Then he called his partner over, and I had to go through the same rigmarole again. That one was from Colorado—and he got a little upset because I placed him. Seemed to think he didn't have an accent of any kind. The only other person there was...a photographer." At the look of stunned disbelief settling over Adam's face, she faltered and ground to a stop.

Finally, breaking the heavy silence, he murmured, "So you put on a real sideshow. Did the photographer happen to ask for your name and address?"

Kaylie stared up at him, considering the ramifications of what she'd said. The sudden memory of the two men, features smeared by stockings, was like a vile presence in the cheerful room. "My God," she said softly, "I really made a mess of it, didn't I? I just never thought. It never occurred to me to take the patrolmen off in a corner and talk to them."

Adam shoved his hands in his back pockets and looked at her. The urge to go to her and haul her into his arms was almost overwhelming. Although he wanted to impress her with the seriousness of the whole thing, he hated seeing the animation slowly leave her face, her fingers unconsciously tightening around the business card she still clutched.

Swearing beneath his breath, he lifted her hand and cupped it between his. The robbery had obviously been her first brush with violence, but she was resilient, and she'd bounced back. She was, he decided, eyeing her returning color, a gutsy lady. Even now, when he'd thrown her precarious position in her face, she wasn't panicking. But she was scared.

Maybe it was all to the good, he told himself harshly. Fear was a good motivator. It instilled caution, and right now she needed plenty of that. Up to this point she hadn't seemed to fathom that she could be in danger. In a way, he could understand. Most people, average people—the lucky ones—grew up in a bubble. If they were very fortunate, the bubble never burst. They never had to confront the darker side of the world.

His life had been different; early experiences with trouble had been part and parcel of the rough side of town he grew up in. The military, then a job in law enforcement, had been more of the same. But things were different now. Now he tried to stay several steps ahead of the barbarians. Prevention, rather than cure, was his current mode of operation.

Old habits died hard, however, and he still had the ability to deal with trouble, whatever its shape or form. And he would use that skill to protect the subdued woman sitting before him. But it wouldn't be easy, he reflected. Her muted air was only a temporary state. She might be down, but she wasn't out. She rebounded like a rubber ball, he reflected wryly, a slight smile curving his lips. Give her a few hours or a good night's sleep, and she'd be back to normal, grumbling about locks and closed doors.

Adam exhaled slowly. He wouldn't have it any other way. He had become addicted to watching her unfettered approach to life. She seemed to greet each new day with optimism and spontaneity, a distinct and intriguing contrast to his own caution and reserve. He wondered if he could instill even a shade of prudence in her. He hoped so, because he had apparently committed himself to insuring both her safety and her freedom.

Opal broke the mood by prosaically collecting the cups and beginning to wash them. "I'm going back to work. You," she said to Kaylie, "should get outside for a while. Go for a nice long walk or something."

Adam rose and tugged Kaylie to her feet. "Good idea. I'll go with you."

She followed him outside with a thoughtful expression. Somehow the idea of two armed criminals wandering around made the private road seem very lonely and far less appealing. She hadn't thought of that before. She'd just assumed that the men were long gone, spending their loot in greener pastures. Of course, she hadn't had Adam around to present the chilling possibilities, either. "I think I'll just roam around the backyard," she told him.

Adam smiled briefly, understanding more than she supposed. "Fine. You can show me whatever we missed on the first tour."

"Come on, then, I'll show you the azaleas that are in bloom." She led him to the far end and stopped before a terraced area bursting with color.

"They're not all azaleas, are they?" Adam asked cautiously.

Kaylie stared at the wall of impatiens, hydrangeas and spirea artistically arranged around the azaleas. Adam, she realized was serious. "It's a good thing the gardener isn't here," she said dryly. "Do you know what any of them are?"

He shook his head. "There aren't any roses," he said definitely.

Grabbing his hand, she led him closer. "I don't know how so many men get through life recognizing only one flower. You've got some catching up to do, so pay attention," she directed.

Kaylie tackled the job with her usual enthusiasm. For the next half hour she led him around the yard, having him sniff various flowers, telling him the names and quizzing him from time to time. She was so busy that she forgot to be afraid. Adam was so pleased that he decided not to tell her that he was allergic to almost every pollen known to man and could no longer breathe through his nose.

"How are you coming with the locks?" They were sitting in an old-fashioned glider swing, and Kaylie asked because she had decided that she now had a vested interest in Adam's progress.

"Windows are all done," he said lazily. "The two doors with broken locks are fixed." And the temporary alarms he had installed on each door would do in a pinch until he got the wiring done.

"What made you go into this line of work?" she asked, pushing against the grass with one foot to keep the swing moving.

"I used to be a cop." He hesitated for so long that she thought he was finished. "I decided that I'd rather prevent break-ins than clean up the mess afterward."

"Is your company a large one?" she asked with genuine curiosity.

"It keeps us jumping," he said laconically.

"Do you deal mainly with business firms?"

"Yeah, but there are more homeowners contacting us all the time. The nicer the house, the more the owners need some sort of security."

"I still find it hard to believe that so many people think it's necessary," she commented. "I'm not putting it down," she said hastily, "but until I moved into my apartment building, I just didn't think of a security system as something the average person needed. My folks didn't have alarms."

He closed his eyes and leaned his head against the back of the swing. "Times change, Kaylie. All it takes is one junkie looking for some quick cash to buy a fix. He can kick the door open in five seconds or less, then help himself to whatever he can sell or trade."

"Kick?" she echoed in surprise. "What ever happened to lock picks and credit cards?"

"We're not talking about Raffles, the gentleman burglar, Kaylie," he said wearily. "For the most part, it's punks and addicts."

She watched a fat bumblebee drunkenly charging into the center of a pink hibiscus. "Maybe it's like that in the big cities. No," she added fairly, "for *sure* in the big cities, I'll give you that. But not out here." At his quizzical look, she said stoutly, "A store robbery has nothing to do with housebreaking. Believe me, *nothing* happens here." Warming to her favorite theme, she continued, poking his arm with a slim finger for emphasis. "I've been staying with Opal for several weeks, and this place is not just low crime, it's *zero* crime."

"For now."

"Forever, I hope." She gestured overhead to the large, upward-spreading branches of a camphor tree. "This place is too beautiful to be ruined by a dose of big-city reality."

Adam nodded, wondering how to bring her back to the subject at hand, that of security measures and her cooperation with them. "So how do you feel about it, now?" he asked, following his own train of thought.

Kaylie stared at him blankly. "About trees?"

He tugged her to her feet and led her back to his favorite part of the property, a narrow path beneath huge old pepper trees. "About locks, alarms and other assorted devices."

"Oh, I'm all for keeping out the bad guys," she assured him. "Especially when there's a possibility that some of them may come looking for me. What I object to is someone who just walks in and takes over—even if it's one of the good guys. Even if it's for my own good. I just have this thing about wanting to be consulted."

"In everything?"

The quietly asked question brought her head up. It sounded innocent enough, but there was something in his tone that set Kaylie's pulse thudding. The gleam in those hazel eyes and his bland expression did nothing to slow it down. The two words, coming from a man who supposedly had nothing but locks and bolts on his mind, conjured up all sorts of surprising images. Hastily blinking away several, she nodded.

"Everything," she agreed briskly, lying through her teeth. The last thing in the world she wanted was a man who asked permission before he touched her, but she'd walk barefoot over a bed of nails before she'd admit it.

Adam propped one shoulder against a gnarled, knobby trunk and reached for one of the lacy leaves. His gaze never left her face.

"I don't believe it," he said flatly. "There are some things that don't require discussion and a vote."

"I'm a firm believer in democracy," she said lightly, trying to ignore the challenge gleaming from behind his lazily lowered lashes. Edging around him, she added, "Even out in the wilds."

Pacing along beside her, Adam reached out and captured her hand in his large one. He nodded ahead at a tangle of trees and said, "That reminds me of the jungle in the old Tarzan movies. Ever watch any of them?"

"Hundreds," she told him enthusiastically, trying and failing to release her hand. "But if you're planning to hold him up as a model of democratic action, you've picked a miserable example. He gave orders and Jane obeyed, right along with the monkeys, lions and elephants."

"A man after my own heart," he murmured.

"It figures."

"He was on his own turf, and he knew which trees to swing from, so he was the logical one to be in charge," Adam said with a grin, provoking her for the sheer joy of watching exasperation flicker in those blue eyes.

"And Jane's part was to scream and wait for help," Kaylie said in disgust. "It took a while, but I finally lost my fascination with loincloths and swinging vines."

Gesturing with his free hand, Adam indicated his narrow hips. "You'll note that there's not a loincloth in sight."

"So there isn't," she said blithely, darting a sneaky, appreciative glance over his muscular frame. "You don't yodel and swing from trees, either. That's a definite step forward. All in all," she finished with an answering grin, "I'd say that today's men are definitely more subtle."

Adam's sudden stillness stopped Kaylie dead. Whatever had been gleaming in his eyes had now been replaced by pure, masculine hunger, and he made no effort to conceal it. His grip shifted to her wrist, and he raised her hand until her fingers rested on his shoulder, and she was close enough to feel the heat of his body.

Kaylie swallowed dryly. "Adam?" The word came out in a whisper, so she cleared her throat and tried again.

His eyes were fixed on her lips as they moved with the sound of his name. Bending his head, he touched them with his in a gentle, questing kiss. His arms wrapped around her, one sliding down until his hand reached the soft flare of her hips; then he drew her into the cradle of his.

Kaylie opened her mouth in protest, and that was all he needed. He kissed her until her breath was gone and her body melted against the hard angles of his. Finally he raised his head, watching drowsy blue eyes emerge as her lashes slowly lifted.

"Subtle?" he murmured. "Maybe. Until we find something that we want. Then you'll find that we haven't changed a bit."

Chapter Four

They *are* from Texas, Detective Hodge. It's up to you whether you believe me or not.'' Kaylie's shrug indicated that she had lost all interest in the subject.

They were sitting in the living room, flanked by Opal and Adam. Adam had, for the most part, remained grimly silent. Opal had distracted the detective, a man in is mid-thirties, by taking copious notes and interrupting whenever she wanted Kaylie to clarify a point. Her interest lay in Kaylie's ability to identify voices rather than in the robbery. She had forgotten her goddaughter's unusual skill and now was entranced with the idea.

The detective, a slim man with brown hair, sat with his legs outstretched, crossed at the ankles. His thoughtful stare was aimed at the toe of one of his glossy shoes. Probably wishing it were a crystal ball, Kaylie thought, taking another peek at his pensive expression. Although the situation was thoroughly exasperating, it did have its amusing side, she reflected, leaning back in her chair.

The morning hadn't started out well for Detective William Hodge. Opal had been the first one to spot him walking across the lawn to the porch stairs. Throwing open the door, she'd beamed a smile at him and said, "Billy! I didn't know they'd send you. How marvelous!" "Billy" had merely smiled at her with a blend of resignation and genuine affection.

"The Hodges moved here when Billy was about ten. He grew up in that yellow house down the road," Opal had explained, waving the man into the living room and performing introductions.

If that hadn't been daunting enough—having tales of boyhood escapades hanging over his head like a sword of Damocles—he'd had to decide whether or not to challenge the presence of both Adam and Opal. After one look at Adam's flinty face, he'd closed his eyes and sighed. Opal, in her inimitable way, had secured her own position in the room.

"I'm so glad you're the one who came, Billy," she had said, grabbing a notebook and sharpened pencil and settling in the chair next to Kaylie. "Don't pay any attention to me; I won't bother you at all. I'm just going to sit here and take a few notes. Kaylie just may have the solution to my next book."

Now the detective's sharp gaze lifted and settled on Kaylie. "It's not that I don't believe you, Miss West. I'm just having a little trouble absorbing the fact that you hear voices the way I see fingerprints."

"Dialects," she corrected, liking his honesty. Detective William Hodge was no dummy. Nor was he a pushover, she decided abruptly. More than likely, he was a man who assessed a situation—such as the present one—and made the best of it. He'd had to choose between being less than kind to Opal or appearing a bit passive. His self-esteem had been strong enough to allow him to decide on the latter.

"Is there much difference?" he asked.

"Just clarifying a point," she told him with a small smile. "Saying that I hear voices makes me sound a little spooky, as if I'm tuned in to the spirit world. When people speak, I hear and can usually identify their regional dialect. It's just that simple."

"Usually?" He pounced on the word like a large cat.

She nodded. "That's right. I'm not a hundred percent perfect. Sometimes I can't get one. But when I can't do it, I'm aware of the fact, and I admit it. I'm not on an ego trip, Detective."

Adam shifted impatiently in his chair.

Before he could come up with one of his unequivocal comments, she rushed on. "In fact, after having the hazards of being a potential witness pointed out to me, I'm not wild about being one."

The detective's thoughtful gaze moved to Adam, then returned to her.

"So, believe me," she plowed on, "I wouldn't be going through this if it weren't true. I'd much rather forget the whole thing."

"Why *are* you sticking your neck out, Miss West?" he asked gently.

Kaylie sighed resignedly. "Generally, I suppose, because I'm cursed with a social conscience. Specifically, because once I realized I had survived with a whole skin, I was furious. I still am. Those two men didn't have the right to rob poor Mr. Jensen, or almost cause Mrs. Grimaldi to have a heart attack. Or to scare the living daylights out of me." Or, once Adam had pointed out the possibility, of making me lie awake at night listening to the creaking timbers of the old house, wondering if someone is trying to get through the locked doors, she added silently.

"Where do you think I spent the early years of my life, Miss West?" The detective's mild question brought her back with a start.

"I thought you'd never ask!" Kaylie grinned at him, ignoring Adam's muttered comment. "You're a Texas boy, too, Mr. Hodge. At least, way back when, you were. From the Panhandle region, I think, probably Lubbock, or further north in Amarillo."

"Well, hell," he said mildly, blinking in surprise. "I came from a little dot on the map smack between them," he admitted. After consulting the toe of his shoe again, he looked up and asked, "What part would you say those two are from?"

"Parts," she said absently. "Billy, the one with the tattoo, is from the Houston area, maybe Harris County. The other one spent a lot of years farther west, probably around San Angelo."

Opal cleared her throat. "That's all well and good, Kaylie, but how do you *know*?" Her slim fingers tightened around the pencil, as if itching to write down something concrete.

"I guess it boils down to the fact that they use the same words we do, but the tune is different," she said, frowning thoughtfully.

"Well, *that* explains it." Opal's gentle sarcasm elicited a look of rueful apology from her goddaughter.

"I'll get you a copy of Professor Wyckoff's book," Kaylie promised. "And he'll loan me some of his tapes, if you want to use them."

"But—"

"Look," she began, knowing that Opal would keep her there all afternoon unless her curiosity was at least partially satisfied. "Every region has its own dialect. In Texas alone, there are four major ones. You listen for things like vowel lilts, tempo, intonation and nasality. It's fascinating. You'll love sinking your teeth into it," she assured the older woman with a grin.

"Well, are you convinced?" Adam aimed the question at the detective.

Hodge cast a speculative glance at him. Adam was leaning back in the large, upholstered chair, radiating leashed energy and watching the entire proceedings with narrowed eyes. He was there, apparently, as a self-appointed watch dog. Masters made no bones about the placement of his priorities: it was the woman first and foremost—his woman. His interest in the robbers was negligible as long as they didn't come within a city block of her. And he obviously intended to stay right at her elbow to make sure they didn't.

"Yup," the detective said laconically, his gaze briefly meeting Adam's. "I'm convinced, and I might just have enough information to pull something interesting about these two out of the computer."

Even while she was answering Opal's insatiable questions, Kaylie had noted the level look exchanged by the two men. It had been brief but comprehensive, she reflected, and had definitely contained an element of recognition. Not that they had met before; she knew they hadn't. It was something more subtle and less definable than that. There was a certain aura of seasoning about them, concealed in different ways under a veneer of civility, but ready to emerge when it was least expected and most needed. She had no doubt that if they tackled a job, they would finish it come hell or high water. And it would be done well.

Filing the interesting conclusion away for later consideration, she asked, "So what do we do now?"

"Nothing." Both men spoke at the same time.

"That is," Hodge amended, "*you* do nothing, and I get back to work. Will you be here if I need you for anything?"

Kaylie nodded. "Sure. At least, Opal and I will be. But I can't speak for Adam," she ended politely.

"I'll be here." His lazy affirmative should have been reassuring, but it came across as more of a subtle threat. "If there's a change in plans, I'll let you know," he told Hodge.

Getting to his feet, the detective said, "Yeah, you do that." Their eyes met in another brief moment of male understanding. "See you soon, Opal," Hodge said, bending over to plant a quick kiss on her cheek before he draped an arm around her shoulder and led her toward the door.

Opal returned a few minutes later, wrapped in thought. "Did you know that cyanide is concentrated in apple seeds?" she said to no one in particular.

"Cyanide?" Adam said, startled.

"Um-hmm. Two or three are harmless, because the body eliminates small doses of it quite easily. A cupful, though, could be fatal. But how on earth would you induce someone to eat an entire cup of the things?" she pondered aloud.

"Edgar?" Kaylie asked, and got an abstracted nod in reply. It always fascinated her to watch Opal change gears and become a Writer. The metamorphosis was quick and complete. One minute she was a small, slender, delightful woman named Opal, and the next she was O. P. Shriver, creator of menace and intrigue. "I thought you had moved on to oleanders."

"He wouldn't eat the leaves I cut up in his salad," Opal said in disgust.

"Did he throw that one away, too?" Adam asked, trying to quell a grin.

"Someone came to the door while he was eating, and he didn't finish his meal. He wasn't hungry. Or so he said. Frankly, *I* think he knows something's up. Mark my words, that man's going to be a problem," she muttered, stalking toward her office.

Adam's puzzled gaze followed her. "I still don't get it," he said, intrigued but disapproving. "She's the writer. She can make him do whatever she wants."

"Tell that to Edgar," Kaylie said dryly. She considered briefly what she had learned about Adam and knew that he wouldn't understand letting such a situation get out of hand. He was not a man who hesitated to use his power, and such a thing wouldn't happen if *he* were writing the book. "Normally, Opal's in total control, with the book plotted out and all systems go. But every now and then a character breaks loose and drives her nuts. And then—" she chuckled in amusement "—it's like watching two chess masters go at it. Opal seems to forget that she's created the person and gets involved in a game of wits with him—or her." Kaylie linked her arm through Adam's and turned toward the door. "If I were a gambler, I'd bet the ranch that we haven't heard the last of Edgar."

Her bright mood lasted until they reached the front yard. Or, more precisely, the mailbox. Next to it, in its bright lavender cylinder, lay the latest edition of the town's semiweekly newspaper. Looking at it as if it were a rattler about to spring, she touched Adam's arm and pointed.

"What's the matter?" His gaze flicked from her face to the object of her pointing finger.

He wasn't slow; she had to give him that. She didn't even have to say a word. He reached out, snagged the paper and tucked it under his arm. "Check the mailbox, then we'll look through this."

"You look while I get this stuff," she urged, pulling a clutch of letters out of the large box. She peered in for a final check and slammed the door. When she turned around, he hadn't touched the paper.

"By now, any normal person would be going through that thing line by line," she pointed out as he placed one large hand on the small of her back and urged her toward the house. "You have absolutely no curiosity."

"What I'm doing is hoping for a miracle, and I'm in no hurry to be disillusioned."

A heavy feeling settled somewhere in the vicinity of her heart. "You're sure that the whole story is going to be in there, aren't you?"

He opened the screen door and ushered her ahead of him. "Human nature being what it is, I'm pretty sure. It's exactly the kind of news a local paper would carry. After all, it's of more interest to the people here than those in a nearby city."

Kaylie dropped the letters on a small table and prodded Adam until he sat on a comfortable wicker couch near the door. She dropped down beside him and grabbed for the paper. When he held it out of her reach, she settled back with a glare.

"Come on," she said in a resigned voice, "open the darn thing. I want to know if I'm doomed to lurk in dark corners for the rest of my life. Or spend my last days behind locked doors. Or fiddling with those panels you're so crazy about. Or—''

"Kaylie.''

The single word was soft and somehow comforting. It seemed to say that he was beside her, and that that was where he would stay as long as he was needed. And as long as he was there, she was safe. She realized with some surprise that, for a person who considered herself independent and self-sufficient, she was finding his unspoken words amazingly comforting.

"Sorry.'' She inhaled deeply. "I tend to dither when I get nervous. But I'm okay now,'' she assured him. "I'm calm as a clam, phlegmatic as a turtle, and placid as a sloth, so now will you, for God's sake, *open that paper* and see if anything's there?''

It didn't take long to find it. A picture, a profile shot of her talking to one of the patrolmen, was on the front page. Beneath it, the identifying text said: "Local writer's houseguest describes robbers.'' Her groan mingled with Adam's soft oath as he turned to the next page. There, two heavily padded columns specified her relationship to Opal and more or less related the entire story.

"I don't know about you,'' she said finally, "but I could have done with fewer details and a lot more discretion.''

Adam folded the paper neatly and placed it on the cushion beside him. "I would have preferred a complete blackout.'' He leaned back and absently reached for her hand, placing it on the sturdy fabric of the jeans that covered his thigh. His warm hand cupped hers, pressing her palm against the hard muscles of his leg.

Bothered by his extended silence, Kaylie peered up at the man beside her. His thoughts had deepened the lines radiating around his eyes and were obviously far from pleasant.

"Those two men will probably never even see this paper," she said, trying to convince herself as well as Adam. "More than likely, they're in Florida or New York by now. It's obvious that they wouldn't hang around here," she said stoutly. "Why would they? They've got the money—or, at least, the jewels," she amended. "It would be the most natural thing in the world for them to get as far away from here as they could. Don't you think so?"

"Hmm?"

Kaylie sighed. Apparently he had given up communicating with the outside world. When Adam thought, she reflected, he seemed to sink into the same sort of semicoma that possessed Opal at her worst. It was as if he gathered all his resources and directed them, like a laser beam, to the problem at hand. Every sense, every muscle and nerve ending, seemed involved in the process. She blinked as her mind made a swift comparison. It was also the way he kissed.

"Nothing important," she said quickly, rattled by the thought. "I just said that the robbers were on their way here and would be tromping up the front steps any minute."

"In that case, we'd better hope they step on the land mine."

Lulled by his matter-of-fact tone, she absently agreed. Then her appalled, "Adam! What are you talking about? What mine?" drew a brief smile from him.

"Just wanted to see if you were paying attention." The faint smile faded even faster than it had dawned. "Kaylie, we've got to look at this logically."

Stifling a groan, she said, "You mean, your way."

"If you can't be logical, then, yes, my way."

"Go ahead," she sighed, knowing that he would, with or without permission.

His hand tightened over hers until she could feel the slight ridges in his jeans and the slide of muscles beneath them. "First of all, we can't assume that they've left town. They could be local talent."

"But—"

"I'm not saying they are—" his voice overrode hers "—just that it's a possibility. And if there's the slightest chance, then we've got to consider the fact when, ah, we make our plans."

"I don't have a plan," she told him, certain that his "we" had been hastily tacked on merely to pacify her. She had been right to be suspicious of the lengthy period of silence, she decided. His strategy was already set, and his part was undoubtedly to issue orders with all the grace and forbearance of Tarzan. No doubt her role, like Jane's, would be to follow them.

His nod seemed to indicate that he would have been surprised if she had developed a plan. "You don't just wait for someone to come and get you, you know. You either set a trap, or move out of the hot zone and keep an eye on things. There's more than one way to handle it."

Well aware that she was out of her element, that desperate robbers were susceptible to neither compromise nor persuasion, Kaylie nodded slowly. "And what are we going to do? If they're really hot on my trail, I'll go along with almost anything, probably up to and including land mines."

She blinked at his sudden daredevil grin. It reeked of masculine anticipation and aggression, but this time it wasn't directed at her. It told her far more than he realized. Adam might have left the turbulence of police work for less troubled waters, but he had definitely missed some of the action!

"You're actually enjoying this," she accused, then couldn't help smiling at the disconcerted look that spread across his face. It didn't last long, but long enough for her to know that she was right.

He shook his head, not convincing her at all. "No, I'm just thinking that those two are in for quite a surprise if they show up."

"How so?"

"They'll expect you to be alone and easy prey," he said matter-of-factly.

Kaylie snatched her hand back and rubbed away an onslaught of goose bumps. "You sure know how to reassure a person," she grumbled. "If that was meant to make me feel better, it missed the mark by a country mile."

This time Adam's warm hand closed over *her* denim-covered thigh, his fingers tightening in a soothing gesture. "You missed the point."

"And that is?" she asked suspiciously, feeling remarkably like a chunk of juicy meat about to be used as bait.

"If they come, they'll be looking for you, right?"

"Right," she said gloomily.

"And they'll find me."

Once again she was startled, this time by his tone of voice. It told her that he had no qualms about facing the two men, that, in fact, he was practically champing at the bit at the prospect. It also reminded her that, should the confrontation come about, he'd be facing two armed men.

"Adam," she began, her voice tentative, "maybe we should call Detective Hodge."

"Why?" he asked blankly.

"You may think you're a one-man army," she said with asperity, "but bullets make big, nasty holes in people. And for some crazy reason, I'd just as soon not have you walking around looking like a sieve."

His chuckle was maddening. So was his sudden hug. "Why, Kaylie, honey, I didn't know you cared."

"I don't," she said stonily, wriggling to escape his warm embrace. "But Opal would never forgive me."

"Opal?"

"Yes, Opal," she snapped, attempting to move one of his large hands from her shoulder. "George would be upset," she said, grasping wildly at straws, "and Opal's very fond of George."

His arm remained on her shoulder, and her body stayed right next to the long, warm length of his. "Speaking of Opal," he said, "we've got to let her know what's going on. I realize that she isn't aware of much besides her book these days, but she has to be prepared."

Kaylie sighed, remembering the older woman's comment that she would feel safe around Adam in any situation. "She'll probably just tell you to do whatever you want to as long as you don't interfere with her writing schedule."

And that wasn't far from wrong.

After they left the porch, Adam collected his toolbox and made the rounds of the five doors. Kaylie headed for the kitchen, telling herself that it wouldn't do any good to brood about the days ahead. "Whatever will be, will be," she muttered, trying to bolster her spirits and failing miserably. She busied herself with planning dinner, then stretched out the preparations as long as possible.

Later, when the three of them gathered in the kitchen to eat, Adam looked down at the baked chicken, rice pilaf, fresh vegetables and bran muffins on the table. A pan of brownies was sitting on the tile counter. Kaylie was obviously a woman who used the kitchen to chase away her particular devils, he thought. And, as a man who rarely came in contact with a home-cooked meal, he couldn't think of a better way for her to release nervous energy. He seated Opal, then held Kaylie's chair for her, his eyes warming as he looked down at her shiny hair. He leaned over and placed a deliberate kiss near the corner of her mouth before he sat down.

Between the clink of cutlery and polite requests for food, Adam attempted to explain the situation to Opal. Kaylie left him to the thankless task, involving herself with a gloomy scenario. Television had a lot to answer for, she decided. Guns, at least those depicted on the screen, seemed rather benign—and quite small. They always tucked neatly into a shoulder holster or hung suspended by some mysterious means between a man's belt and the small of his back. The pistols held by the robbers had looked very nasty and very large.

"Are you listening to me, Opal?" Adam slanted an irritated glance at Kaylie and was not measurably soothed when she smiled blandly and scooped up another forkful of rice.

"Of course I am," she said, blinking up at him. "Robbers, you said. But I don't have any in the book I'm working on. You must be thinking of *Waterway*. It's about a robbery in the French Quarter in New Orleans. Or *The Valley*. It takes place around here." She waved a hand to include the encompassing area. "The thief took chips. Silicon, not potato. Which reminds me," she said, turning to Kaylie, "the rice is delicious."

Adam inhaled deeply. "Not fictional robbers, Opal, real ones. And they just might be coming here."

"Here?" Her head tilted questioningly. "Whatever for?"

"Because your local paper said Kaylie can identify them."

"I suppose she can," Opal allowed judiciously. "At least, in a way." She turned back to Kaylie. "What we need," she told her, "is a plan. You don't just sit around and wait for things like that to happen."

"We have one," Adam said. "But it may involve packing up and getting out of here," he said to Opal, ignoring Kaylie's start.

"You two can go. They're not after me."

Adam shook his head in a way that informed both women that the issue was not negotiable. "No way, lady."

"But if I don't know where you're going, I couldn't very well tell them, even if they did show up."

"They wouldn't believe you." He picked up his knife and neatly cut off a piece of chicken. "But it doesn't matter. I'm not leaving you behind."

The two women looked at each other, their eyes widening in silent communication. The matter was apparently settled.

Conversation during the remainder of the meal centered around Opal's definition of packing light. Adam's expression grew increasingly forbidding.

"My computer has to go," Opal stated, but when a vein in Adam's temple began to throb, she relented. "I have a portable. I suppose that would do."

The evening passed. That was about all Kaylie could say for it. The drapes had been drawn, and she prowled restlessly around the living room. Opal was in her office, deciding what reference material she would take if the exodus were mandated.

Adam watched Kaylie pace around the room, the greenish gold of his eyes all but concealed behind lazily lowered lids. He sat quietly in a corner chair, where he had a view of the entire room.

"Kaylie." His soft voice sounded loud in the still room.

The quiet word brought her head up.

"You're wearing yourself out. Why don't you go upstairs to bed?"

Her pent-up breath came out in a big sigh. Looking at her watch, she nodded and said, "I suppose I should. I'm going to wear a hole in the rug if I keep this up."

He got up and walked over to her. Kaylie didn't want to touch the work-roughened palm extended to her. She didn't want to step forward when two arms tightened around her. She didn't want to lift her face to his, and, most of all, she had no intention of letting her lips soften beneath the touch of his. But she did.

With a surprised murmur of protest, she slid her hands along his chest until she felt the strong thud of his heart. She spread her fingers and pressed, gently at first, then with more force. When he slowly dropped his arms, she turned, went up two steps, then stopped with her hand on the rail. As she looked down at him, a slight, self-conscious smile curved her lips. "Uh, you *will* lock the doors, won't you, Adam?"

Kaylie optimistically shed her clothes and dropped a shortie nightgown over her head. Two hours later she looked at the bedside clock and the twisted sheets trailing over her bed, then groaned. Unconsciously, she had been waiting for the sound of Adam's firm tread as he passed her door and headed for his room. But he still had not come upstairs when she finally drifted off to sleep.

Minutes or hours later, the piercing wail of an alarm shattered the silence of the night and brought Kaylie to her feet. She threw open her door and ran down the hall to pound on Opal's.

"Come in."

Opening Opal's door, Kaylie found the older woman tying the belt of her bathrobe firmly around her waist. "That must be one of Adam's alarms," she said calmly. "I suppose this means we'll be leaving."

"Adam! He may be hurt!" Kaylie turned and headed for the stairs.

"Where do you think you're going?" Adam's hard voice stopped her on the third tread. "Woman, don't you *ever* go running head-on into trouble." His gaze took in the sheer gown. "Especially dressed like that. Go get packed. We're getting out of here before they decide to come back."

Kaylie gazed down at the tall, rumpled, hard-faced, bare-chested man and swallowed dryly. "Adam," she said in quiet warning, "your loincloth is showing."

Chapter Five

It was less than an hour later when Kaylie dumped two packed suitcases at the head of the stairs and ran down to the first floor.

Now maybe she'd have a chance to voice a few of the words that were buzzing around inside her head like a swarm of angry bees. Exactly who did Adam Masters think he was to send her to her room like a child? Not that she had argued once she followed the line of his gaze to her nearly transparent nightgown. But that was beside the point. She wanted to know if the robbers had actually appeared, or if there was some other explanation for the alarm. Any number of things could have set it off. She'd read once that it was possible for animals to trip the sensors.

Adam hadn't allowed her to utter any of her queries. Instead, he'd given her one hour to pack, told her that he'd answer her questions when she had done so, and swung back into the living room.

Kaylie was trying hard not to be unreasonable. She *was* grateful that he was there, that he had taken the matter of her protection squarely on his own broad shoulders. She'd be a fool not to value the safety factor his presence added. But—and it was a mighty big *but*— she did not want to be treated like an idiot child in the process. Was it asking too much to be consulted once in a while? To have him ask for her opinion? Or even to tell her what was going on? Of course it wasn't. Only a thoroughly arbitrary person—like Adam Masters— would think so!

"Adam?" she called, as her foot left the bottom stair.

"In here."

She followed the sound of his voice into the living room. He was sitting in the large, upholstered chair he seemed to favor, speaking softly into the telephone and writing notes in a pad that was balanced on the arm of the chair. His hair looked as if it had been combed with his fingers, with one dark lock resting on his forehead, but at least he had his shirt back on, she noted with relief. Well, mostly on. It was unbuttoned a good part of the way down, but at this point she'd take whatever she could get. A confrontation with him would be difficult at any time, but almost impossible when he was dressed as he had been earlier, with low-slung jeans and a mat of crisp, dark hair covering slabs of muscle on a massive chest. It would have been like negotiating with Conan the Barbarian.

"Got that?" he was asking. "Good. I'll leave it in your hands. Yeah, sure. You too." After he cradled the receiver, he looked up and said, "That was George. He's coming down to supervise the work here at the house while we're gone."

"What—"

Cutting her off with an upraised hand, he said, "One more call, then we'll talk." He pulled a card from his wallet, glanced at it, then reached for the telephone and poked out a series of numbers.

"Who are you calling?"

"Hodge." He hunched his shoulder, tucked the phone in the resulting curve and flipped to another page of the small notepad.

"You're not waking him up in the middle of the night!"

He looked at his watch. "You're right, I'm not. It's closer to morning."

"Adam!"

"He gave me his number in case something like this hap—" He broke off and said, "Hodge? Adam Masters. Yeah. Visitors, two of them." A pause. "No. My alarm worked too well. Scared the—" he looked at Kaylie and stopped in midstream "—uh, pants off them, and they took off in a van." He cocked his head, listening. "No. I couldn't see the license or the color. Dark is the best I can do."

He listened impatiently, and his next words were even more clipped. "I'm taking them to my place in the mountains. While we're gone, my partner is coming down to install some hardware. No, there's no phone in the cabin, but you can leave a message at this number." He gave the detective the location of the cabin and the telephone number. "We'll be leaving within the hour. Sure, you do that. I will."

He replaced the receiver and turned to Kaylie. "He said he'd be in touch if he collects your two friends and needs you to identify them."

She dropped down into the chair beside his. "Good. That's one call that can't come any too soon." His expression wasn't encouraging, but she took a deep breath and firmly changed the subject. "Adam, we need to discuss a few things. First of all, I really do appreciate the fact that you're helping me. I don't know where I'd be if you weren't."

"You'd be in the van that took off like a scalded cat," he said bluntly.

"But in spite of my gratitude," she continued through gritted teeth, "I can't go on like this."

"Like what?"

He wasn't going to make it easy, she thought with a scowl, wishing that he would button his shirt. "Like following orders and wondering what the heck is going on. I made a better partner than I do a subordinate. You keep saying that we're going to talk, but by the time we get around to it, you've made all the decisions. Your part of the conversation is nothing but a series of orders."

Adam sighed sharply and leaned his head back against the chair, not even trying to hide his impatience. "In my books, Kaylie, a partner is someone who has equal experience, expertise or ability. When I *consult* with someone—" he leaned heavily on the word she had used the day before "—it's usually because they have information that I need. What do you have to offer?"

Kaylie lowered her lids and worked on not being intimidated. Her blue eyes were snapping when she opened them. "So far, not a thing," she said briskly, "and you know it. All I'm saying is that I function better when I know what I'm doing!"

He turned to her, hazel eyes gleaming with determination behind lowered lashes. "Then let me tell you what's been happening. I stayed downstairs tonight because I figured that if these jokers were local, they'd read the paper and head over here sometime after dark. Two men came, ran into the alarm and took right off again. I think it would be stretching coincidence a bit far to assume that it was just some junkies who randomly picked this house to break into, wouldn't you?''

She nodded reluctantly.

"And I would say that your good ole boys will be back, wouldn't you?''

She nodded again.

"So while they're busy making their plans, let me tell you what you'll be doing. You'll be getting in my car and going to my cabin in the Sierras, where you'll stay until this mess is cleared up. Do you have any objections to that?'' His tone informed her that she'd better not have.

"Yes."

"What the hell do you mean, yes?''

"I'm not leaving my car behind."

Adam suddenly realized the difference between losing a battle and winning the war. He didn't like her little sardine can. In his opinion, it shouldn't be allowed on the road, but if that was what it took to get her out of the line of fire, then so be it. What the hell, he thought philosophically, the tension easing from his body, I can always put it out of commission when we get there.

"Ouch, that hurt!" Kaylie picked herself up off the thick mat and rubbed her bottom. Her red shorts, while allowing her to move freely, supplied no protective padding. "I just want to know one thing." She panted, scowling at Adam, who didn't even have the courtesy to pretend that he was breathing hard.

"What's that?"

"Why, after a week of doing nothing more strenuous than strolling through the woods and swimming, did you decide that it was time to slowly break every bone in my body?" She waited as he took his own sweet time answering. There was a humorous glint in his eyes, and he was looking as innocent as a pirate on the prowl could look.

"Because it was just a few minutes ago that you told me you'd been trained in self-defense." He turned her around and brushed off the back of her shorts.

Kaylie shook off his lingering hand with a waspish flip of her wrist. "I also told you it had been a while since I took the class."

"I just wanted to see how rusty you were."

She blew back a strand of hair with an exasperated puff. "Well, now you know. I creak."

"Come on. Let's try it again."

"Me and my big mouth," she groaned, grinning despite herself. He was determined to whip her into shape in one lesson, even if it killed her. And he was approaching the project with the total concentration she had become accustomed to. "Next time I'll know better."

"What did you expect me to do?" he asked with genuine interest, as if he were fascinated by the way her mind worked. "Just let it go at that? I had to find out if you could actually use what you learned."

"Well, I didn't expect to be dragged down into your torture chamber," she retorted. "We were having a *conversation*, Adam. You know, one of those innocuous things where you say something, then I respond? If all goes well, you say something else, and so do I. The average person doesn't jump up in the middle of a phrase, drag another person into a padded cell and start manhandling him—or her."

She glanced around the room, which really served as a gym. If the equipment was any indication, Adam, who was a fiend for keeping in shape, was prepared for any event, up to and including a small siege. She had seen the gym the day they arrived, when Adam had shown her and Opal around the cabin. Actually, "cabin" was a misnomer. What Adam had was a beautiful redwood and glass home perched on the side of a mountain, with conveniences that would have satisfied a delegation of the world's pickiest women.

"Come on." Adam extended a long arm, snagged her shoulder and brought her close to him. Turning her around so her back was to him, he held her throat with his forearm and said, "Okay, dump me."

A twist and a grunt later, Kaylie was once more flat on her back looking up at him. He stood there, feet slightly apart, hands resting on his hips, a speculative look in his eyes. "You know what the problem is?" he said seriously. "You just don't have the killer instinct."

"I promise you—" Kaylie wheezed "—if I ever get my body off this floor, I'll murder you."

He grinned as she slowly bent her right knee and waggled her foot. Her lashes brushed her cheek, and she drew in a deep breath. Her thoughtful gaze settled on his face.

"Adam," she said carefully, "I think there's something wrong with my back." With extreme caution, she slid her leg down until it was flat on the mat.

Swearing softly, Adam leaned over her.

"Don't touch me!"

Adam froze, his hand extended. With painful slow-ness, Kaylie reached for his hand, her face a mask of concentration.

He landed with a satisfying thunk a few feet away. Kaylie turned her head until her cheek brushed the mat. Adam was flat on his back, his head almost even with hers. Gleaming blue eyes locked with enigmatic hazel ones.

"Gotcha," she murmured softly, a satisfied smile curving her lips.

"Is there anything wrong with your back?" His pen-sive gaze never left her face.

Her smile grew broader. "What do you think?"

Her lashes lowered in lazy contentment, and Adam moved. It wasn't until his knees straddled her thighs that she suspected something had gone wrong. When his hands clasped her wrists and anchored them to the mat on either side of her head, she was sure of it.

"Now, Adam," she began, laughing helplessly at his intent expression.

"Like I said," he pointed out mildly, "no killer in-stinct. You should have finished me while you had the chance."

"I promise," she gasped, "next time I'll do you in with a chop to your Adam's apple—Adam."

His knees tightened, holding her squirming body still, as he looked down at her face. "It's too late. I've got you now."

It had been too late for her that first day, when he had followed her into Opal's kitchen. She didn't seem to understand that, nor the fact that he wasn't about to let her go. She had talked about picking up the threads of her life when this episode was over. Of returning to her apartment, finding another job, perhaps going into business for herself. The only thing she didn't talk about was whether or not a man was waiting for her in San Francisco. There couldn't be, he decided. Not an important one, at any rate, or he wouldn't have let her go for so long.

No, so far she failed to understand that what was growing between them didn't fall into the "temporary" category. Hell, she didn't even realize that there *was* something growing! She treated him like a cousin most of the time. Before she accepted the fact that something vital, something permanent, was developing, she needed to know him, to understand how his mind worked—and that would take time. He knew he couldn't rush the process, and he would allow her all the time she needed. As long as it was within reason.

That was what this last week had been all about: time—given and taken. Once they arrived at the cabin, it hadn't taken her long to revert to her former way of life. Windows and doors had been thrown open and left that way. Apparently twenty-four hours of apprehension hadn't been enough to put a noticeable dent in her trust mechanism. Out of sight, out of mind, seemed to be her credo. It all evened out, though, because he doubled his vigilance and hardly let her out of his sight. And he managed to do it without saying a word.

Subtle, he thought with a wry smile. After all these years, that was what he was becoming. It wasn't easy, but then, was anything worthwhile easy to achieve? he wondered. For the price of biting back certain words and a bit of tact, he was beginning to win Kaylie's trust. Not only was she losing that wary expression when she looked at him, but she had even quit vetting every word before she spoke. It was a fair accomplishment for a week's hard work.

What had brought on that slight smile? Kaylie wondered, watching Adam's lips curve. He was a hard nut to crack, she decided for the hundredth time. Somewhere along the way he'd forgotten how to enjoy life. She'd invested more time and effort on him this last week than she had done when she'd sold a particularly tough thirty-unit complex, and what did she have to show for it? Once that she could remember, *once*, he'd laughed. It had been genuine, spontaneous laughter that had her helplessly joining in, but *once*, for heaven's sake! Several times he'd grinned at her, and it had taken everything she had to keep from turning tail and running. His grins were not domesticated, and they had shaken her right down to her tingling toes.

And he was more relaxed; the lines of his face were softer, gentling his earlier razor-sharp image. She could take credit for that, she decided. Of course, he still didn't take her all that seriously. Usually, when he looked at her, the expression in his eyes was indulgent. And more than once she'd caught him watching her with a baffled look, apparently wondering how she survived in the world as he knew it. But at the moment, after having been tossed on his backside, he was trying to decide if her expertise had been a fluke or if she had suddenly recalled her instructor's every word. She closed her eyes to conceal the satisfaction that was oozing from every pore of her body. It didn't do to rub these things in too obviously.

It was the second time she closed her eyes on him, and the second mistake she made.

"Adam?" Her eyes opened with an almost audible snap. In a single movement he had slipped to her side and rolled to his back, swinging her atop him, fitting her frame to the warmth of his. His legs anchored hers, pinning her lower body to his, as she looked down at him and absorbed his untamed smile.

"Hmm?" His fingers were laced behind his head, and he was watching her, his smile turning into one of those dangerously lazy grins, as Kaylie tried to find a safe place to put her hands.

It wasn't an easy thing to do. If they slid down to his shoulders, every square inch of her body would be plastered to his. If they settled on his chest, every beat of his heart would be transmitted through them. She arched her back in an attempt to shift her weight and found that the movement only drove her hips closer to his. She also discovered that he wasn't nearly as relaxed as he pretended to be, at least, not all of him. Finally, in desperation, she settled for propping her elbows on his chest and resting her chin in her hands.

"What's this all about?" she asked.

"Your next lesson." His green-gold eyes smiled up at her.

"I never did anything like this in class," she told him, widening her eyes in mock innocence. "Am I in the advanced group already?"

As he was about to answer, they heard the front door open. Adam released her legs, gently tumbled her to the mat and was on his feet and extending a hand down to her before the door closed. She could feel his sudden tension dissipate when Opal called out.

"Adam? Kaylie?"

"We're down here, Opal," he called. "Coming right up." His gaze lingered on Kaylie's face for a beat before he gestured for her to precede him up the stairs. She went, wondering if she had just escaped that well-known "fate worse than death" and, if so, why she felt such a pang of regret.

"What on earth have you got?" Kaylie had stopped in the doorway, looking at Opal, who was all but lost beneath a sea of foliage. Adam drew to a halt behind her, watching from over her shoulder.

"Come here and help me," Opal directed briskly. When Kaylie reached for some of the longer branches, she said, "No, I'll hang on to these. Spread some newspapers on the table." When that was done to her satisfaction, she dumped the messy armful on them.

Adam silently estimated the length of the various sprays. "If that's for a flower arrangement," he said doubtfully, "I don't have anything to put it in."

Opal's oblique glance informed him that she had no time to waste on such frivolities. "Research, Adam," she said absently, staring down at the leafy stems. After placing a pair of pruning clippers on the counter, she shed her gloves and long-sleeved overshirt.

"These are from an oleander bush," she said, "so be careful. My reference book says the entire plant is toxic. One leaf is sufficient to kill an adult, so once you touch them, don't put your hands to your mouth."

"Then why are we going to touch them?" Kaylie asked in a reasonable tone.

Opal rummaged through a drawer and pulled out a large brown paper bag. She opened it and dropped it on the floor beside the table. "Because we're going to make skewers out of them."

Adam and Kaylie stared first at her, then at each other. "Why?" she asked for both of them.

Opal was already busily tearing leaves off a shoot. When it was denuded, she bent it, scowled, and muttered that it was too flimsy. After tossing it in the paper bag, she reached for another one. Glancing at her two fascinated observers, she demanded, "Are you going to help me or not? But if you have any cuts on your hands, wear gloves or something."

"How about broken bones?" Kaylie asked, wincing as she sat down on the cushioned chair and took a branch.

Opal pointed at the table. "Work," she said succinctly.

With a shrug, Adam reached for the heaviest branch. After a moment's consideration he pulled a small knife out of his pocket, opened it and began lopping off the leaves.

"Be sure and wash that when you finish."

"Yes, ma'am."

"I don't know," Kaylie said doubtfully, looking at the frayed end of her bare stick. "You couldn't puncture anyone with this."

"Let me have it," Adam said, reaching for it. With a few economical movements, he whittled the end to a point.

Opal nodded, pleased with the results. "That's fine. You've got the wrong idea, though. I'm not going to stab anyone with them. I'm arranging a barbecue for Edgar. I just wanted to see how hard it would be to make these. And if they'd work for shish kabob. My book said they can be fatal if used as skewers."

Adam looked up. "I thought he didn't eat meat."

"He doesn't. It's a vegetarian shish kabob. It should work, don't you think?"

They both nodded in agreement.

"Good. Then that's all I need." She began dumping leaves and sticks in the paper bag. In a short time the bag and papers were disposed of, and they all scrubbed their hands. Opal turned toward the room she had appropriated for an office. "This time," she told them confidently, "he'll be stopped dead in his tracks."

Kaylie smiled faintly as she closed the door behind her. "That sounds like one of those 'famous last words' statements." She dropped back down into the chair and groaned as her bottom hit the cushion. "It's all your fault," she told him, squinting her eyes and trying to look severe.

"Want me to rub it for you?"

"What I want from you," she said, pointedly ignoring his offer, "is the assurance that your hot water tank is large enough for me to take a hot bath that may well last into the afternoon."

"You can use all you want; I've got solar heating. Does that mean you don't need any help?"

She extended her hand. "Only to get out of this chair."

After what he considered a reasonable time, Adam knocked briskly on the bathroom door. "Are you decent?"

"I think so."

He opened the door and came to an abrupt halt. "You are," he assured her, staring at the mounds of frothy bubbles that covered her from shoulders to ankles. Her head, with hair pinned haphazardly atop it, rested on the curved edge of the tub. At the other end, beneath the faucets, her feet broke through the iridescent beads.

Lazily wiggling her toes, Kaylie let out a contented sigh. One hand broke through the bubbles in a laconic wave. "Hi. Just here for a visit?"

"I brought you something." He lifted a tall glass of iced tea, the instant, artificially sweetened, lemon-flavored stuff she drank by the gallon.

"You may have just saved my life," she decided after a thoughtful pause. "I was dying of thirst but not quite ready to forsake my therapy."

A dark brow rose inquiringly. "Therapy?"

"Um-hmm. This is where I do my heavy-duty relaxing. I've also come up with quite a few creative concepts for my job."

Adam folded his arms across his chest and leaned back against the steamy wall. He didn't consider himself an inordinately imaginative man, but at the moment he was having a few very creative concepts himself.

Kaylie wasn't built along voluptuous lines. She was gently rounded in all of the right places. Her body was much like her face—neither classically beautiful, nor perfect, but, somehow, for him, just...absolutely right. Add to that her enthusiasm and vibrant grace, he reflected, and you had a lethal combination. She had a fresh, unconscious sensuality that brought him to his knees.

And that was exactly where he'd like to be right now, he thought. On his knees beside that oval tub, wrapping his arms around her silky body. Lifting her, watching the glistening beads evaporate, then taking her to the large bed in his room.

Tension crackled in the air until even Kaylie's bemused senses stirred. What was going through his head? she wondered, unable to decipher the look on his face. In the next instant she decided that she was better off not knowing. This was no fresh-faced, boy-next-door type she had towering above her. What she had on her hands was totally male, tough and dangerous.

Bypassing the flickering speculation in his green gaze, she switched her gaze to her toes. The cool air that he had brought in with him was having a decided effect on her creamy cover. Rubbing one foot over the other, she cleared her throat. "Uh, Adam?"

"Yeah?"

"My bubbles."

His gaze skimmed over the frothy shield. "What about them?"

"I think they're popping." She took a quick swallow of tea.

He checked again, this time more slowly. "You may be right."

"I'm sure I am," she said firmly.

"Want me to run some more hot water?"

"No!" The last thing she wanted was to have him come any closer than he already was.

"Your toes are getting wrinkled."

Kaylie glared up at him. Blast him, she thought, he was really enjoying this! But some small part of her was pleased to see the glimmer of humor in his eyes, even if it was at her expense. He was doing much better at smiling these days.

"Overexposure to hot water does it every time," she informed him. "It happens right before they fall off. Adam, will you move your big feet out of here!" And take your long legs, narrow hips and broad shoulders along with them, she added silently.

He surged away from the wall, bringing a large towel with him. Dangling it above her, he said, "Want this?"

"Please." He dropped it in her outstretched hand.

"By the way, you'd better brace yourself," he warned almost whimsically.

Surreptitiously she eyed the thinning sheet of froth. It was breaking up; it now resembled ice floes adrift in the ocean. "For what?"

"Edgar gave his skewer to another vegetarian, and the wrong man died. Opal is calling for a council of war."

Kaylie groaned, scowling at the gorgeous line of his back until the door closed behind him.

Chapter Six

Adam? Where are you?"

Adam looked up from the O. P. Shriver mystery he was reading as Kaylie appeared in the front doorway.

"Oh, there you are." She kicked off her sandals, stepped through the doorway onto the oak floor and looked at him curiously. Adam had a vast store of energy, and she rarely caught him loafing. "What are you doing?"

He held up Opal's book, *The Train to Nowhere*, so she could see its cover.

"You got hooked, didn't you?" she asked, amusement lurking in her blue eyes.

He nodded, his gaze drawn back to the printed page.

"You won't be putting it down for the rest of the day," she told him. "Actually, the timing couldn't be better. Opal and I are going into Mariposa, and I don't know when we'll be back." Watching him, Kaylie saw something she hadn't seen since they left Saratoga. His hazel-green eyes cooled until they resembled a winter brook, heavily iced around the edges, and she knew she would not be pleased with what he was about to say.

"No, Kaylie." The words were soft, but definite.

"No?" she repeated blankly. "No, *what*?"

"No, you're not going into Mariposa."

There was a longish pause while Kaylie stared at him in disbelief. She took a deep breath, and when she spoke, it was with slow, distinct emphasis, her teeth almost biting off the words. "Adam, I hate to remind you of this, but I'm not a child and you're not my father. I am chained neither to this cabin nor to you. And I don't need your permission to do anything!" Then, just in case he had failed to get the message, she added, "You can't keep me from going."

Something coiled in his eyes, something cold and flat and more than a bit intimidating. Something that made her blink, take a deep breath and fleetingly wonder if the trip was worth a mammoth confrontation. But anger and a feeling of If-I-don't-draw-the-line-somewhere-I'll-be-in-big-trouble took over. "Let's put it this way," she said, narrowing her eyes. "You'd better not try to stop me."

Adam silently cursed his quick, tactless tongue. Eight days of patient, ground-laying work had just blown up in his face as a result of several thoughtless words. "You came up here for your safety," he reminded her evenly, laying aside the book.

She nodded. "You're right. I came because there was a specific threat in Saratoga. I hardly need to point out that it doesn't exist here. I haven't gone any farther than the store down the road since I've been here, and I'm not going to hibernate or completely isolate myself for however long it takes to settle this case." She scowled at his unrelenting grimness. "We're just going to the Mariposa County History Center and the library so Opal can look up a few things. What on earth could be more innocent? I didn't say that we were heading for New York or San Francisco, for heaven's sake. And I'll personally guarantee that there won't be a reporter in sight." She turned and slid into her sandals. "We'll use common sense, but I refuse to become paranoid about this."

Without waiting for his response, she swung out of the room, her short skirt brushing the tops of her knees at every step. "Opal?" she called. "Are you ready?"

Moments later, the yellow sports car started with a low rumble. Kaylie zipped it backwards down the driveway to the road, hit the brakes, swung it around and aimed it for town.

"Are we in a hurry?" Opal asked, staring at the speedometer needle as it nosed its way well beyond the speed limit.

Kaylie exhaled sharply, suddenly aware that she had been holding her breath, waiting for Adam to do precisely what she had told him he couldn't: stop her. The expression in his narrowed eyes had been distinctly unsettling, but a quick look in the rearview mirror reassured her, and her foot eased up slightly on the accelerator.

As they sped through the sparsely settled rural area near the southern tip of Highway 49, Opal said, "I gather that Adam wasn't too pleased?"

"You got it," Kaylie said, taking another involuntary peek at the mirror.

"The way you're keeping tabs on the road back there, you act like you're expecting a rear attack by Attila the Hun."

"It wouldn't surprise me a bit. That's exactly the way he looked when I left." She glanced unseeingly at rolling hills dotted with heavy brush, young pine trees and venerable oaks. "I thought I was making some headway with him this past week," she said in disgust. "We actually talked to each other instead of playing his favorite game."

Opal's face brightened with pleasure as she examined a sleepy little ranch house nestled in a grove of sycamore. "What game?" she asked absently.

"The one where he snaps out an order and waits for me to follow it." She took her eyes off the road long enough to look at her godmother. "Am I expecting too much?" she asked plaintively. "Am I being unreasonable?" Turning her attention back to the curving road, she said, "All I want the man to do is explain himself, to share his thoughts, to treat me as a sensible, rational human being."

"George once told me that Adam acts first and discusses later."

"If someone were pointing a gun at my head, I'd appreciate that quality enormously," Kaylie told her as they neared the small town laid out along the slopes and floor of the slender valley formed by the Mariposa Creek.

Opal took it all in, captivated by the steep, narrow streets and the combination of old and new architecture. "I've got to explore this place," she announced, as if Kaylie intended to drive through town without stopping.

Kaylie nodded, still absorbed in her own dark thoughts. "By the look on his face, you would have thought I was bringing you in for a TV interview or something," she muttered. She signaled for a right turn at the History Center, nosed the car through the parking lot's sloping entry and pulled into the first available slot. Getting out of the car, she looked around and smiled for the first time since she'd left the cabin.

Kaylie loved small old towns. They usually came equipped with large old houses and friendly people. "Too bad Adam didn't come with us," she told Opal. "He would have been reassured. He might even break down and admit that nothing could possibly happen here."

Wincing at the screech of the tires, Adam stood at the window and watched Kaylie back the car out of the drive with her usual verve. He tensed, waiting for the sound of a shattering windshield or for a thump, which would indicate that her car had tipped over into the shallow depression at the side of the road. He had found himself listening for those sounds more times than he cared to count in the past week, since she was the one who usually volunteered to run down to the small grocery store to do the shopping. Finally he had decided that impetuous types like Kaylie must be under the mystical protection of a special guardian angel. Or, more likely, a host of them.

When imminent disaster receded, he dropped back down into the chair and picked up Opal's book, absently running a finger down its spine. She could get hurt in that little tin bucket; it would be no protection at all in an accident. As far as that went, he reflected, the way she smiled at perfect strangers and struck up conversations with them wasn't much safer. He dropped the book on the table beside him and went into the kitchen for a beer. Pulling the tab on the can, he scowled as he thought of the myriad ways in which she courted disaster.

Actually, he silently admitted, if she had to take Opal anywhere, it might as well be Mariposa. The little town in the middle of nowhere, with its population of just over twelve hundred, wasn't exactly sin city. Of course, during the summer thousands of tourists flowed through, either bound for, or returning from, Yosemite Valley. But even someone as paranoid as Kaylie accused him of being couldn't be certain that those two creeps would be among them.

They had no reason to be. Before he had hustled the two women out of the house, he had made sure that the van was nowhere in the area. Once the three of them were on the road, he'd dropped behind Kaylie's car to ensure that they weren't followed. They hadn't been; he would stake his life on that. And back in Saratoga, only Hodge and George knew where the three of them were, and neither man was likely to satisfy the curious. So, regardless of how anxious those two were to get their hands on Kaylie, they had no reason to be milling around Mariposa looking for her. With that thought he took another can of beer into the living room, settled back with Opal's book and tried to convince himself that he wasn't listening for the rumbling motor of a little yellow car.

After spending a fascinating hour in the History Center and vowing to return soon, the women walked across the foyer into the library. Kaylie settled down in a wooden chair near the door and prepared to enjoy herself as Opal zeroed in on the dark-haired librarian. At such times the older woman never volunteered the information that she was a writer, at least, not at first.

Kaylie often wondered whether it was because she assumed that everyone knew, or if she didn't think it was important, or if she simply never thought about it. Whatever the reason, the fact that she was doing research for a novel usually emerged only after a period of distinct confusion—a period that Kaylie had learned to regard with deep appreciation.

The main problem with her godmother's approach, Kaylie had decided several years earlier, was that Opal didn't gradually lead up to things. She just followed her own train of thought and assumed that everyone else would do the same. Unfortunately, it rarely worked out that way.

The librarian looked up and smiled pleasantly at the petite, gray-haired woman standing by the desk. "May I help you?"

Opal returned the smile. "Yes. I want to kill Edgar with a cupful of apple seeds, but I can't figure out how to make him eat them. Do you have any books on poisons that might help me?"

The younger woman's smile froze on her face. "Apple seeds?" she repeated cautiously.

Opal's nod was one of deep satisfaction. "Enough cyanide in them to kill an elephant." After a moment's consideration, she carefully amended her statement. "Maybe not an elephant, but a mule."

The librarian's eyes shifted from left to right, then back again. "Cyanide." She tested the word carefully. "Of course."

"So if you'll just tell me where the poison books are, I'll go see if any of them have any suggestions. *My* book certainly didn't."

The woman's reaction reminded Kaylie of poor Mr. Jensen, who'd had an alarm button practically at his elbow and no opportunity to use it until it was too late.

"Your book?"

Opal nodded again. "A very good reference book. It told me the seeds were poisonous, but it bogged down when it came to any practical advice."

Kaylie noted that the librarian, after a quick glance around the empty room, had once again allowed her gaze to settle on Opal's face and apparently decided that it was safe to try to reason with her. "Perhaps you need to think about it, find another method of dealing with the problem," she said gently.

Opal shook her head. "No, it has to be this way. He wouldn't eat the castor beans, and he killed off a very nice old gentleman when he gave away the oleander skewer that I prepared for him."

"Killed?"

Dropping down into the chair next to the desk, Opal nodded. "That was the last straw. I had spent days setting that man up as a perfect red herring, and just like that—" Opal snapped her fingers beneath the astonished woman's nose "—Edgar did him in."

The woman's fascinated gaze never left Opal's face. "What did the police say?"

"They're still asking questions." She leaned against the back of the chair, her expression softly triumphant. "But someone burned the skewer, so there's no murder weapon."

"Aren't you going to tell them?"

Opal looked at her, stunned. "Do I look crazy?"

The woman's eyes widened, and she shook her head hastily. "No. Absolutely not."

"They'll find out in time. But I've got to get that blasted cupful of seeds down Edgar before they do. Now, are you going to help me or not? I've got a deadline to meet."

A speculative looked flitted across the librarian's face.

Kaylie could almost see the words *red herring* and *deadline* being considered, chewed and digested. She got up, caught Opal's eye, waggled her fingers in good-bye and headed for the door. The fun was over, at least for now.

She walked briskly toward the center of town, keeping on a dirt path that ran parallel to the busy road. After a block or so she crossed some invisible line, and sidewalks materialized, leading her past bakeries, bookstores and antique havens. She had a couple of hours to kill while Opal pored through books in the library, and she couldn't think of a better way to do it than by sampling what the town had to offer.

Fifty minutes later, sitting in a small café nursing a glass of iced tea, she made a silent admission. Window-shopping, for once, had palled quickly. She found herself disregarding summer clothing for the doubtful fascination of a hardware display of power tools. Her thoughts had slid to Adam, imagining the smooth play of shoulder muscles as he easily controlled the rugged pieces of metal and chrome—as easily as he had shifted her weight against his heated body when they lay on the padded mat. With a groan, she had walked on, stopping at the window of a men's store, complete with a male mannequin. That had led to images of Adam in a slim-cut bathing suit that emphasized his long legs, slim hips and muscular chest. Then she'd mentally sprinkled crisp, dark hair on the vision's chest, hair that had turned into a narrow trail somewhere around his navel, disappeared into the midnight blue trunks and reappeared with a vengeance on muscular thighs.

Involuntarily she thought of the moment in Opal's backyard when he had tugged her into his arms. It hadn't been a simple matter of lips meeting. As a matter of fact, there had been nothing simple or casual about it—it had the same blunt honesty that characterized all his actions. When Adam Masters kissed, his whole body got into the act—and she had been aware of every inch of it. Her hands had rested on wide shoulders, unable to decide if they should push him away or slide to the back of his neck. Her breasts had been gently crushed against a broad, rock-hard chest, and, farther down, his large hand had settled in the small of her back, pressing her against the solid evidence of his arousal. An arousal he made no attempt to conceal. An arousal he made sure that she—

"More iced tea, ma'am?" A teenager stood beside her, holding a full pitcher poised over her glass.

She transferred her gaze from the inch of crushed ice in the bottom of the glass to the waitress's face. "Yes, please."

Enough of X-rated Adam Masters, she told herself firmly, lifting the cold glass and downing half of its contents. True, she had never before reacted so physically to a man.

And probably never would again, her built-in devil's advocate commented.

But there were other things to be considered.

Like what?

Like the fact that he was not the kind of man she needed or wanted in her life.

Do we have to be so intense about this? that little voice asked.

Yes. The man, aside from his physical attributes, is impossible.

What do you want, for heaven's sake?

A man who understands what give-and-take is all about. A man who doesn't use a sledgehammer to kill a gnat. A man who knows that some things are negotiable. A man who presents the advantages of a situation and then uses a bit of persuasion.

You've been in sales too long.

Had she? Kaylie wondered, dropping a tip on the table and taking her check up to the cashier. Had she really? She had definitely been in real estate for too long, but sales? Real estate, with its high-stress factor and obligatory vigilance, had finally taken its toll, resulting in a bad case of burnout. Some people thrived on the life, but in her case, aside from the money when business was good, there seemed to be two cons for every pro. The paperwork and accompanying telephone calls were backbreaking.

But sales? That was different. What she hoped to find, once she ended her visit with Opal and began looking, was a field where she could match people and products without the hassles of escrow, loans and contingencies of other sales. She might even go into business for herself, she thought as she walked back toward the library. After four years of pretty much being her own boss, independence, along with a healthy bank balance, ranked high on her list of priorities.

No, sales work had been good for her. Her training had been excellent and enhanced her self-esteem. Of all the things she had learned, reducing conflict when dealing with others was probably the most valuable.

Negotiating, she found, seemed to fall into two categories: hard and soft. In a very short time she had discovered that the softer approach was more suited to her personality. She automatically regarded participants as friends, tried to avoid a contest of wills, and made offers. That system worked fine unless she came up against a hardball player like Adam, who considered participants as adversaries, did whatever it took to *win* a contest of wills, and made threats.

She had no illusions about Adam. He was going to be a hard nut to crack. And she wasn't asking for the impossible from the man, she reminded herself. All she wanted was a little reciprocity, a little mutual consideration. She didn't tell him how to occupy every minute of every hour, so why on earth couldn't he allow her the same freedom? An emergency was different. She would do whatever he ordered without question—at least until the all clear sounded. No, it wasn't his credentials she questioned—she was sure that he could handle trouble in any shape or form. It was his attitude that drove her crazy. Surely he didn't believe that danger lurked behind the pine trees around his cabin or in any of the small towns nearby.

Still brooding about a certain six-foot-plus package of trouble, Kaylie walked back into the library and stopped dead. The quiet room had been transformed into a veritable anthill of activity. Folding chairs had been brought out and placed in rows, and women filled the room to overflowing. A few men sat quietly, waiting.

Kaylie spotted Opal in the center of the room, surrounded by a cluster of women. With a sinking feeling that grew stronger each moment, she edged her way over to Opal.

Opal looked up with a smile and excused herself. "Guess what?" she said, leading Kaylie to a quiet corner.

"I'm afraid to. Opal, you're not going to talk to these people, are you?"

Looking back at the rows of chairs, she nodded. "It seems so."

Heaving a what-did-I-ever-do-to-deserve-this sigh, Kaylie said, "I've only been gone an hour. What happened?"

"Once Miss Grace found out—"

"Who's Miss Grace?"

"The librarian. Once she discovered that she had O. P. Shriver in here doing research, she called a few friends who enjoy mysteries. They called a few more, and they called—"

"Don't tell me," Kaylie said in resignation. "A few more." She stared at the steady stream of people flowing through the door. "Do you have any idea what Adam's going to say about this?"

Opal grimaced. "Probably the same thing that George would."

"I don't suppose you'd like to explain to the librarian that you shouldn't be making any public appearances right now?" She knew it was a losing battle when she saw a "the show must go on" gleam in Opal's eyes.

"No, I wouldn't. Do you see any harm in doing this?"

"Well, no," Kaylie admitted, torn between honesty and the knowledge that she'd rather face an angry rattler than an angry Adam. "But I don't have a death wish, either. You know he's determined to make it look like we've vanished from the face of the earth."

Opal extended a hand and placed it on Kaylie's arm. "And he's right. Those men weren't playing when they tried to break in. But I truly believe that we left them behind. If I thought there was any danger to you, I wouldn't even consider doing this. But there's no way on earth that news of a small, friendly talk like this will find its way to Saratoga."

"I know." Kaylie bent down and kissed Opal on the cheek. Nudging her gently toward the lectern that two men were sliding into place, she murmured, "Have fun." Then, gloomily considering all the ramifications of Murphy's Law, she looked around, discovered that all the seats had been taken and dropped down into the chair beside the librarian's desk.

Opal's talk was chatty and informal. She described her life as an author and responded to the inevitable questions about where she got her ideas and which came first, the chicken or the egg—or, in her case, the plot or the characters. An hour later she had answered all the questions and smiled several times for a plump lady with a small camera.

Kaylie stirred uneasily. "Who's that?" she asked Miss Grace.

"The program chairman for one of the cultural groups. She keeps a scrapbook."

"Oh."

Opal autographed some books that a few enterprising souls had grabbed from their bookshelves at home and joined Kaylie. "Well, that was an unexpected pleasure, but I still haven't solved my problem."

"What's that?"

"Apple seeds. And how to get them down Edgar."

The librarian spoke up, pointing to the book near Opal's purse. "Maybe you'll find something in there, or you can always go with the rhododendrons. The symptoms are certainly gory enough."

"I'm not looking for gore," Opal said firmly. "Just effectiveness."

"I think we'd better get going," Kaylie interrupted, fully aware that, given half a chance, Opal would turn back to the stacks and start looking for information on another exotic herb or plant.

On the way back to the cabin, Kaylie asked, "What do you think? Do we tell Adam or not?"

"Not."

"Guilty conscience?"

"Not at all. It's just ... kinder."

"And smarter."

"There's absolutely no reason to worry him about something so insignificant."

"I couldn't agree more."

"I suppose he really would be upset."

"Furious might be a more appropriate word."

"Oh dear."

"Indeed."

"You're not very comforting."

"Misery loves company."

Opal broke the thoughtful silence. "You've been with me for several weeks now."

"I didn't think you'd noticed," Kaylie said with a grin.

"What about your job? You've never stayed longer than a weekend for the last several years because you always had escrows pending or whatever they do."

"I chucked it."

"Why? I thought you liked the work and the people."

"I did, most of the time. My biggest satisfaction came from matching people up with their dream houses. If that was all the job called for, I'd never leave it. But the rest of it, the paperwork, finding lenders, having people back out of deals at the last moment, coping with the hatchet jobs of other agents, is a real pain in the tush. I won't miss any of that."

Opal squirmed within the confines of the seat belt, reaching up to adjust the strap that was doing its best to sever her jugular. "What are you going to do?"

Kaylie shrugged. "Run away from robbers. Loaf."

"I'm serious," Opal said, a slight frown bringing her brows closer together. "You're too energetic to just sit around doing nothing."

"Actually," Kaylie said, slowing down as she spotted a green and white car ahead of her, "I'm considering several things." Opal's silence was encouraging. "I invested some money several years ago when I sold a couple of multiple units, so I could buy into a business. Maybe a franchise of some sort. Or—and this is something that really interests me—I could develop a sales training class and sell it to corporations."

"I thought you had to have degrees and impressive credentials to do things like that." Opal loosened the shoulder strap until it looped down near her elbow.

"That's going to do you a lot of good if we get in an accident," Kaylie observed, slanting a glance at the sagging belt.

"Is it any better to be decapitated by the strap? These things were obviously designed by men who gave no thought to small women. Anyway, what about the degrees, etcetera?"

"I don't know," Kaylie said slowly. "I have the qualifications. I'm good. No," she amended, "I'm *very* good. I've been training the new agents in our office for the last couple of years, and our sales have been right up at the top. But you have a good point. People are impressed by titles and degrees.''

"I like the idea. You should give it some serious thought.''

"I will,'' Kaylie promised, turning into the driveway and pulling to a stop beside the cabin. She shrugged out of the seat belt and turned to Opal. "You can't imagine what a challenge it is to take some throwback to Genghis Khan and teach him the elements of negotiation, the art of gentle persuasion.''

"It sounds wonderful,'' Opal agreed. "You could start making notes, at least. Too bad you don't have someone to practice on up here. It would at least keep things from getting too dull.''

As the sound of the motor died, Adam came out the front door, stood on the deck and stared down at the women. Kaylie's gaze met Opal's for a brief moment, and the women's lips curved up in identical smiles.

"Speak of the devil,'' Kaylie murmured.

Chapter Seven

"That's not exactly what I meant," Kaylie said with genuine amusement as they sped down the road in Adam's Bronco, a heavy, four-wheel drive vehicle that he kept at the cabin. The scarf covering her hair fluttered in the breeze coming through the open windows. "I don't think you've been taking me seriously this last week. How am I going to turn you into a salesman if you don't listen?"

"I don't want to be a salesman," he said reasonably, a slight smile lifting the corners of his mouth. He was more relaxed than she had ever seen him, Kaylie thought contentedly, accepting a certain amount of credit for the change.

"All right, forget salesman. How about being an effective representative of your business?"

"I'm that already. Without all your fancy games."

Kaylie sighed and audibly counted to ten. "How many potential customers do you lose because you aren't willing to take the time to show them how one of your widgets works? How often do you hand them an estimate, then go back to the office and wait for their call?'' His fingers tightened on the steering wheel, and Kaylie had the impression that he would rather have pressed them over her lips.

Without taking his eyes off the road, Adam said, ''Our reputation has spread by word of mouth. Practically everyone who comes to us is a referral.''

''Great! That's the way it should be,'' she said promptly. ''But what about the ones who need a little prodding, a little persuasion? How many of them slip through your fingers?''

His shrug indicated that he couldn't care less. ''If we got them all, we'd probably have more business than we could handle.''

''Aw, gee,'' Kaylie said in mock sympathy. ''Then you'd have to expand and hire more people. Look,'' she argued, a glint of amusement lighting her eyes, ''it's simply a matter of finding out what the customer needs and wants. People buy benefits, not features.''

''Is that supposed to mean something to me?'' he asked, enjoying her persistence. Of course, he admitted silently, he'd be pleased by almost anything that kept her attention centered on him.

''Think about it for a minute,'' she ordered briskly. ''Say your widget has ten special features and your client needs or wants five of them. Five of them become benefits, the others don't. Your job is to sell the benefits. It's really very simple,'' she ended politely.

''And how do I do that?''

''You haven't been listening,'' she reminded him. ''By asking questions.''

He groaned. ''We're back to games again.''

"Fortunately for you," she interrupted, pushing her outsize sunglasses back up on her nose and hanging on to the slipping scarf, "Mariposa's right around the curve. There's not enough time for me to win the argument, so we'll pick up where we left off on the way home."

Adam parked in approximately the same place Kaylie had the week before. He grasped Kaylie's hand in his as they met in front of the huge blue car. Rather than comb her flyaway hair, she had simply tightened the scarf and once again pushed up the dark glasses. "After I return the book Opal borrowed, we can browse through the History Center. You'll love it," she assured him. "I probably won't be able to drag you out."

It wasn't until they walked up the stairs of the small building that the perils of taking Adam into the library occurred to Kaylie. His reaction two weeks ago when he had heard that she'd allowed herself to be interviewed by the police while a reporter snapped pictures had been bad enough, she remembered with a wince. Once he'd settled down, though, he seemed to have written it off as abysmal ignorance on her part. But he wouldn't be so forbearing a second time. Good lord, no, he certainly wouldn't! Suddenly she realized just how pleasant the past week had been and knew that if she wanted their peaceful coexistence to continue, a meeting between him and Miss Grace was to be avoided at all costs.

"Adam," she said hurriedly, stopping inside the foyer and pointing to the left, "why don't you go in and start soaking up history?" With a nod to the right, she added, "I'll return the book and be right with you."

He looked down at their clasped hands and deliberately laced his fingers through hers. "There's no rush. I'll go with you."

Before she could protest, a voice that she had once thought pleasant sounded in her ears like the crack of doom.

"Oh, there you are. Did the book help?" Miss Grace waggled her fingers in greeting.

Kaylie dredged up a smile. "I think so. Thank you so much for all your help. This is my friend, Adam Masters, and we're going into the other room to look around. Bye." She dropped the book into the librarian's hand and turned toward the door, towing a surprised Adam along with her.

"Think nothing of it. I've got another one that should help her coming in on our county truck in about an hour. It's a small return for what Opal did. Everyone enjoyed it so much."

The words floated behind them and for one, fleeting moment, Kaylie thought she had managed to get away. Unfortunately for her, Adam's reflexes were quicker than hers. His fingers closed around her arm and none too gently pulled her to a stop. Bringing her along with him, he turned and walked back into the library, aiming a charming smile at Miss Grace.

"Exactly what did Opal do?" he asked with interest.

"Adam, I'm sure you'd be more interested in the stuff in the other room," Kaylie interrupted nervously.

He locked his arm around her waist and held her easily at his side. "As soon as I hear what Opal did to earn such appreciation," he said, directing another smile at the intrigued librarian.

"You mean her talk?" she asked.

"Talk," he repeated. "To people?" He looked down at Kaylie. "Is that what I mean?"

She nodded, speechless.

He turned back to the other woman. "How many people?"

"Oh, the room was full," she said, in what Kaylie considered gross exaggeration. "There were chairs all over the place. Must have been thirty or forty, wouldn't you say?" She turned to Kaylie for confirmation.

Looking up at Adam's expressionless face, she nodded weakly in agreement. "I suppose."

"I don't imagine your local newspaper sent a photographer along for the occasion, did they?" he asked, far too softly.

Miss Grace shook her head in regret, then brightened. "But we got pictures," she told him helpfully. "Myrtle Olivet—the program chairman I told you about," she reminded Kaylie, "brought her camera."

Adam took a deep breath and exhaled slowly. "What did she do with the pictures?" Kaylie winced as his voice grew even softer.

"She gave us a couple for our bulletin board and the rest went into her scrapbook."

Kaylie slanted a look up at Adam, mutely sending the message that he was worried about nothing, absolutely nothing, and what did he think she was, a fool?

"Except for the ones that she sent with the news release," the librarian added belatedly.

"Where did that go?" Adam's voice, quiet as it was, easily overrode Kaylie's groan.

"Myrtle thought Opal might like a little publicity in her home town and took the time to send a copy to the Saratoga newspaper."

Kaylie's horrified gaze froze on Adam's face, registering the fact that without moving a muscle he had changed from an amiable companion to a...a what? A hunter? A protector? A... Swiftly she rejected the im-

age that flashed into her mind, then slowly brought it
back out for inspection. Cold-blooded killer? At this
precise moment she wasn't placing any bets. Anger was
emanating from him like sheets of gray icy rain, and he
seemed capable of anything. Kaylie was surprised that
the librarian hadn't picked up on it and sought the ref-
uge of her desk. *She* certainly would have if Adam
hadn't tightened his hold on her wrist until it resembled a death grip.

"Thank you," he murmured to Miss Grace before he
turned and took the few steps back into the foyer.

"Don't forget to come back for the book," she
called.

"Adam," Kaylie said, stunned by the sudden change
in him, "I'm sorry. The whole thing just got out of
hand, and it seemed so innocent."

He stopped before they reached the main door, apparently lost in thought. "Later, Kaylie," he said absently, staring down at the hand he had wrapped around
her wrist as if it contained the answer to some obscure
question. After a pause that seemed to last forever, his
head lifted, and his cool, near-green gaze met hers.

"If that program woman knows her job and got the
pictures developed and the release written right away,
what day do you think it would hit the paper in Saratoga?"

Kaylie started to speak, stopped to clear her throat
and began again. "Yesterday," she said faintly. "But,
Adam, we don't even know that the editor would consider it worth printing. More than likely, he wouldn't,"
she added hopefully.

"But maybe he did, and just possibly your two
friends read it," he replied in a flat voice. "You just

can't wish these guys away, Kaylie. You have to consider all the possibilities and assume the worst."

"What an awful way to live."

"It's called survival, and it gives us a chance to keep one step ahead of them. It also keeps the advantage in our court."

"What advantage?" she asked bleakly.

"Actually, there are several." He tapped his chest, saying, "I'm the main one. They don't even know I exist. They didn't see me at Opal's house, since they tripped the alarm before I got to them. Then, I spotted their van. They don't know about that. There's also the matter of their voices. If they come after us, and I'm assuming they will, they have to talk to each other. And you can ID their voices, right?"

"Right. But they've seen me. They could pick me out of a crowd long before I could hear them."

"Not if you keep those goggles on," he said, sliding the sunglasses back into place with a long finger. "And if you keep that scarf over your head. Your hair is a dead giveaway." He fingered a long strand that streamed across her shoulder like an amber ribbon.

"I could cut it," she offered thoughtfully.

"The hell you will!"

Kaylie looked up, blinking in pleased surprise. So far he had reacted more strongly to that suggestion than he had to the entire situation. Wrapping that interesting observation away for further consideration, she pulled her thoughts back to the present. "So what do we do now?"

His hooded glance was full of speculation. "How brave are you feeling?"

"Not very," she admitted. "Those guys are scary. They're...mean," she faltered, aware that she wasn't doing a very good job of explaining just how terrified she had been in the jewelry store.

Adam grinned, that macho, anticipatory grin that drove her wild. "Honey, if we're going to talk *mean*, I've got more than a slight edge on them."

"But they've got guns," she explained earnestly, convinced that he was still vastly underestimating the competition.

He glanced obliquely down at her, his expression enigmatic. He didn't say a word.

"*Adam*. Do you mean—"

"How do you feel about taking a walk?" He leaned forward, opening the door behind her, then stopped to slide her glasses up one last time before he herded her outside.

"Walk?" she protested, "I'm not going anywhere until you tell—"

"Walk," he repeated, urging her outside and threading his fingers through hers.

"Where?" she asked, shrugging in defeat and taking a skipping step to catch up with him. Stopping him was like trying to halt a mudslide in California after a solid week of rain. He slowed down, matching his stride to her shorter one, keeping her close to his side.

He gestured ahead. "Toward town, where we can blend in with the rest of the tourists. And where I can look for vans, and you can listen to voices. But first I want to call Bill Hodge and see if my instincts are on target, if anything actually came out in the paper."

Kaylie followed him to a public telephone, muttering, "That's the most sensible thing I've heard you say all day." She nudged against him, hoping to hear something, but all she accomplished was to get herself tugged closer, with Adam's arm clamped around her

waist. Watching his face, she knew when he went omi-
nously quiet that what he was hearing was not good
news.

Adam listened, saying, "Yeah, um-hmm, okay,
sure," at intervals. After an extended pause he said,
"You do that. I'll keep in touch." He replaced the receiver in the cradle, took Kaylie's hand again and
headed once more for the center of town. "It was in the
paper."

After a moment spent grasping at straws, she asked
cravenly, "What about the local police?"

He stepped behind her, his hand at her waist, while a
cluster of approaching tourists broke rank and flowed
unevenly around them. "I wouldn't count on them too
much," he commented, when they were once again on
their way. "Hodge said he'd give them a call and let
them know what was going on, but with the lack of
hard evidence, I doubt if they'll move very fast."

"Lack? How much do they want?"

"More than we've got. Which isn't a hell of a lot,"
he added with maddening logic. "We have you saying
that you can identify some voices. We have two men in
a van who tried to break into Opal's house, which might
or might not be a coincidence. We have the possibility
that two men might show up here looking for us. Our
instincts tell us that they're the same ones, but we don't
have much to back up our feelings. No, I think we're
pretty much on our own, at least for now."

He drew her to a halt, squinting from the glare of the
bright, hot sun on the sidewalk. After sliding on a pair
of aviator-type sunglasses, he touched her shoulder, and
they walked on. The better to spot vans without being
caught, Kaylie thought with a shudder, deciding once
again that she didn't like any part of this. It was one

thing to read about a fictional heroine, intelligent and gutsy, leaping from one perilous venture to another without even mussing her hair. It was another thing entirely to be thrust willy-nilly into such an undertaking totally against one's better judgment.

"I hate to say this, but I'm going to anyway," Kaylie said as they reached the far end of town. "If those two *do* show up, the only lead they have is the library, which is on the other side of town. Of course, it isn't all that far away, but still, they wouldn't be here, browsing through stores or admiring old buildings. If I were them, I'd be back there—" she pointed in the opposite direction "—asking Miss Grace a few casual questions about Opal and her goddaughter."

He looked down at her, his lips curving in a small teasing smile. "If I sell out to George, want to start a detective agency?" Ignoring her muttered comment, he added, "You're right, but there weren't any vans around the place when we came out, so I thought we might as well stretch our legs. Let's get something to eat, then head back. We can look at some of the stuff outside the Center, so it won't be too obvious if we hang around for a while."

"I don't think it would matter anyway. People come and go there all day long."

They found a small restaurant and placed their orders. Before Adam bit into an enormous hamburger, he said, "Tell me about the robbery again. Did you talk to those two characters at all?"

"No." She shoved some french fries around her plate and wondered how he could eat at a time like this. "Not a word."

He swallowed and made appreciative noises. "How about Jensen? Did you talk to him?"

"While the robbers were there? No."

"Any time at all. After the robbery?"

"I already told you what I did before and during it. But, after? I'm not sure." She absently took a bite of her ham sandwich and chewed thoughtfully. "Just chitchat, while we were waiting for the police to get everything they needed. You know the kind of stuff. He asked me if I was staying long, that sort of thing."

"And what did you say?"

Kaylie shrugged. "I said the usual things about the town. It wasn't hard; Saratoga's a nice place. In fact, I told him if he could promise that I wouldn't be robbed blind, I might start a business there myself." She took a swallow of iced tea. "As you can see, it wasn't world-shaking conversation, just idle talk to pass the time."

Adam finished his hamburger and eyed the untouched half of her sandwich with interest. "Are you going to eat that?"

She transferred it to his plate. "You probably never gain an ounce," she said. "Not only is it unfair, it's depressing." When she saw that she was being ignored, her thoughts went back to Saratoga. "All the green is absolutely dizzying after living in the city for so long. And people just let nature have its way. They live on *land* rather than lots, and there aren't any fences marking property lines. It's all done with rows of trees or huge, overgrown bushes and shrubs."

She stopped suddenly. "Adam? Are you there?" He was staring at the steaming coffee in his cup and probably hadn't heard a word, she decided, moving back her plate and scrabbling through her bag for a lipstick.

"Tighten your scarf," he said briskly, coming out of his trance. "It's time to hit the street again. And keep your glasses on."

His nerves must be made of cast iron, she thought, glancing sideways at him and feeling just a tad resentful. He was acting as if he were going on a picnic, while she felt her stomach tightening with every step that took them closer to the library. "Don't things like this make you nervous?"

He gave it some thought as he scanned the passing cars. "No," he said simply.

"That's not natural! Why not? We could be facing armed killers down there! How do you know what sort of—" she stopped, searching for an appropriate word to cover all the appalling possibilities "—stuff we'll be mixed up in?"

He rubbed his thumb soothingly along the back of her hand. "Maybe they won't be there. Maybe they never will be there. Maybe I blew the whole thing out of proportion."

She looked up hopefully. "Do you really think so?"

He shook his head. "No. I'm just saying that anything is possible. And I've been through enough... stuff—" he hesitated before settling on her choice of word "—that I've learned not to waste my ammunition before the target comes in sight."

Kaylie kept one foot moving in front of the other, hoping that he was using the word figuratively, not literally. Then, after a moment's reflection, she decided that he'd meant precisely what he'd said. As an ex-Green Beret and ex-cop, he must have experienced more than his share of violence and had who knew how many opportunities to wield weapons. Instead of being cheered by his undoubted expertise, she surprised herself by responding with a fierce pang of regret for the man who somewhere along the way had had his ideals replaced by a massive dose of realism. Her fingers closed around his and squeezed softly.

Adam looked down inquiringly, tilting his head. Kaylie's gaze got as far as his chin before she decided that she felt a little too vulnerable to meet that undiluted blast of inquiring hazel. Shaking her head, she kept on walking—even when he lifted her hand to his mouth and softly kissed the tip of each finger.

They were almost at the end of the block when he said, "Hey, look at this!" Her heart slammed in alarm until she belatedly recognized that his tone was one of unbridled pleasure.

"Don't do that to me!" she wailed softly. "I thought you had seen them."

"How could I?" he asked in a reasonable tone. "Neither one of us knows what they look like. No, I was talking about this." He pointed to a colorful poster stapled to a telephone pole. "There's a county fair starting next week."

Kaylie grinned at the sight of her "killer" yearning over the poster. He looked like a kid with his nose pressed against the window of a toy shop. "I take it you like fairs."

"Love them." He gave the poster one last longing look and turned away.

"What do you like the most?"

"The games. The noise. The friendly atmosphere. The rides. The—"

"I like to throw balls at the wooden milk bottles," she told him, ruthlessly interrupting his litany of wonders.

He gave her one of those maddening masculine glances. "Do you ever hit anything?"

She raised her brows with an air of lofty contempt. "Do I *hit* anything? I'll have you know, I'm the terror of the fairways. The concessionaires probably have my name written down in a little black book."

He made a tsking noise with his tongue. "I'm surprised you admit it."

"Not that kind of black book, idiot. One that bans people from playing, one that lists the people who break the bank."

"You're that good, huh?"

"I'm that good. I was the only girl in my neighborhood who was allowed to play baseball with the boys. They fought like tigers to have me on their team."

"Because they liked your legs?" he hazarded with a grin, eyeing the long, graceful limbs appreciatively.

"My throwing arm," she said succinctly. "I was the pitcher."

He nodded at a second poster. "Want to go? I'll win a teddy bear for you."

"It's a date," she told him, her lips curving in a grin to match his. "And we'll see who does the winning."

He stopped and looked down at her, his green-gold eyes never leaving her face. "It's a date," he repeated slowly, his voice heavy with satisfaction. Sliding her glasses back into place, he said, "We'd better get going."

When they left the bright sunshine for the darker interior of the building, Kaylie looked cautiously in both directions, for all the world, Adam thought, as if she expected someone to leap out of a corner and yell "Boo!"

"Psst! Kaylie!"

Kaylie jumped, looked over her shoulder and saw Miss Grace wiggling a beckoning forefinger. Adam followed her into the near-empty library.

"Did your friends find you?"

Kaylie swallowed dryly and noticed that the simple question had accelerated her heartbeat to twice its normal rate. She shook her head, and, over the roar of the blood thundering through her veins, heard Adam questioning the woman.

"Two men," the librarian told him. "No, they didn't say who they were, just that they saw Myrtle's article about Opal in the Saratoga paper, knew that Kaylie was with Opal, and, since they were coming this way, thought they'd stop in and ask for directions to her place. Kaylie's, that is, not Myrtle's. Won't Myrtle be pleased that the paper printed her article? They don't very often, you know, especially if they get the story after the fact."

"Did you tell them where they could find Kaylie?" Adam asked, stopping the flow of words.

"No," she said in surprise, "I couldn't. I don't know where she's staying. Besides, I had a feeling that two personable young men might not be welcome," she added, pointedly examining Adam's hand possessively clamped at Kaylie's waist.

"They're not," he assured her.

"Well, in that case, I'm sorry, but I told them I expected her back in an hour or so to pick up a book."

"Do me a favor?" Adam asked her. Kaylie caught just the tail end of the smile he directed at the librarian and was dazzled. If he exerted that much energy on potential customers, she thought with a blink, he could sell heaters in Death Valley in July. She wasn't a bit surprised at the librarian's dazed tone.

"What?"

"If they come back, don't tell them we're here. Let us find them and decide if we want to invite them over."

All the world loves a lover, and Miss Grace was no exception, if her enthusiastic agreement was any indication. Adam inspected Kaylie's glasses one last time and led her outside, stopping so quickly that she barged right into him. Following the direction of his gaze, she didn't ask the question forming on her lips. There, parked near Adam's car, was a black van with a red thunderbolt on the side.

Adam looked at the license plate. "It's time to go hunting."

Kaylie hardly recognized his voice. It matched the cold, hard, flat look in his eyes. She shivered, grateful that he was on her side. "What do we do?" she whispered.

"We walk and try to look like tourists. And you listen."

They started on the north side of the building, strolling past mining exhibits, pausing a moment by the arrastra, a primitive circular, mule-powered device for crushing ore. They walked by the Indian village, and by the time they reached the south side, Kaylie was looking at the ground, concentrating on the different voices as they passed one group of visitors and approached another.

"By God, look at the size of that sucker."

"What is it?"

"A stamp mill. They crushed gold-bearing quartz with it, then saved the gold."

"How do you know?"

"It says so on the sign."

Kaylie's nails dug into the arm Adam had wrapped around her waist. She was close enough for him to feel her body stiffen, all the way down to her blue running shoes. Drawing her to a halt, he bent his head and touched his lips to her cheek.

"Bingo?" he whispered.

She nodded.

"Take a good look at them as we go by."

Kaylie was so sure the two crooks could see behind her glasses and beneath the scarf that it took every ounce of courage she could dredge up to lift her eyes from the ground. It was almost anticlimactic when two ordinary men came into her line of vision. They were dressed in jeans and knit shirts, and one had sandy hair, the other dark brown. And both their voices had traces of a Texas accent.

Drawing a deep breath, Kaylie wrapped her arm around Adam's waist and turned away with him.

"I think we ought to go out in front and keep our eyes open," said a familiar, soft twangy voice behind her. And two pairs of feet scuffed on the dirt track behind them.

They passed the entrance, and the two bringing up the rear stopped beneath a shady tree. Adam and Kaylie were turning onto the walk leading to the parking lot when Miss Grace stepped outside.

"Yoo-hoo, Kaylie, you forgot Opal's book!"

Chapter Eight

Kaylie!" The librarian's voice carried across the entryway with appalling clarity. "Opal's going to need this!"

Adam's hand tightened on Kaylie's arm. "Don't turn around."

It was good advice, Kaylie acknowledged, terrific advice, but it came just a beat too late. At the sound of her name, her stride had faltered and she'd instinctively looked over her shoulder. A second later she heartily wished that she hadn't. The two men lounging in the shade stiffened and began ambling in her direction.

Adam swore softly. "Come on!"

If his short command wasn't enough encouragement for her to break into a trot, the brisk tattoo of the men's footsteps on the ground behind them gave her the final incentive. Adam had his key out by the time they reached the Bronco. He opened his door, stuffed Kay-

lie in and rushed in behind her. "Buckle up!" he ordered, inserting the key and reaching for his seat belt at
the same time. The vehicle came to life with a throb-
bing rumble, and Adam had it out on the road before
Kaylie had taken a deep breath.

"You think they'll come after us?"

"Take a look."

Kaylie glanced over her shoulder just in time to see
the black van thunder out of the driveway and turn in
their direction. It didn't look as if the driver was paying any more attention to the speed limit than Adam
was.

"Can't you go any faster?" she asked. Then, resolv-
ing not to watch that black speck get any larger, she
turned back and stared with morbid fascination at the
dashboard. The speedometer needle was leaning heavily
to the right.

"Adam, you could get a ticket!"

Shaking his head, he took his eyes from the road for
a second to see her eyes fixed on the gauge. "You think
of the damnedest things. Right now, I'd welcome the
sight of a black-and-white."

Taking another quick look behind her, Kaylie winced.
"I don't like this." The words were a heroic piece of
understatement.

"That makes two of us."

"Yeah, but I don't like it because I'm scared. I have
a strong feeling that if I weren't along, you'd be enjoying yourself."

"Hang on," he ordered a few minutes later, taking a
sharp right onto a narrow, two-lane road.

"I don't think you're going to find the police out
here," she gasped, clinging to the door handle as the
Bronco bucked and bumped over deep ruts in the road.

"No, but think how much fun our friends behind us are going to have."

"Yeah," she said faintly, watching as acres of tawny brush and small trees slid by in a blur. *She* hadn't had so much fun since she broke out in hives.

Scraggly bushes and water-deprived trees grew in a tangle right down to the side of the crumbling asphalt. As the road spiraled upward, Adam was unable to see more than twenty or thirty feet ahead. He slowed down at a hairpin curve and took another sharp right, gearing down to climb a steep hill. They surged to the top in a snarl of power and stopped on the proverbial dime, the nose of the Bronco tilted high against the sky.

Kaylie swung her head around in surprise. "This is no time to stop and admire the view, Adam. Those men are right behind us!"

"We've got a slight problem," he said laconically, looking ahead through the windshield.

Struggling to pull herself higher in the seat, she said, "At this angle, I can't see anywhere but up into the air. What's the matter?"

"We ran out of road," he said simply.

Kaylie's eyes narrowed in a glare. "Not funny, Adam. No one just runs out of road. Besides, I thought this was an off-road vehicle."

"It is, but it needs something to move on." Ignoring her look of patent disbelief, he pointed a finger ahead of them and swung it around to the right. "Just in front of us is a drop of about two hundred feet. That—" he pointed to the hill rising on their left "—is almost straight up."

Kaylie's eyes widened. "You mean that we have to—"

He nodded at the unfinished question, swinging the Bronco in a tight circle. "Yep, go back down."

"But they're—"

"Coming up," he finished with another nod. "And that means we've got to get back to the last sharp turn before they do. They had to slow down considerably when they hit this road, but they're only a couple of minutes behind us." With no more warning than that, he shot the Bronco down the hill, its wheels barely skimming the road.

"Adam."

"Hold on."

Kaylie was trying to do just that, but her main concern was her stomach. She had never suffered from car sickness, but then, she had never driven with someone who had apparently cut his teeth on the set of *Smoky and the Bandit*, she reflected morosely. When they landed at the bottom in one piece, she opened her eyes and watched as Adam pulled far enough off the road to settle behind an ugly, overgrown mass of leaves that seemed to have dedicated itself to the production of nasty looking thorns.

"I think I'm going to be sick," she informed him.

"*No one* throws up in this car." The way he said it made a believer out of her. She was definitely not going to be the first, even if she had to ride the rest of the way with her head hanging out the window.

"What do we do for an encore?" she asked, taking a shaky breath. "Fly over the van when it comes in sight?" He *was* enjoying this, she decided after a quick glance. His body was practically humming with energy and adrenaline, while hers was almost mortally deprived of oxygen. To be fair, she reminded herself, this mess was none of his doing. He was under no obligation to save her neck, but as long as he was, she thought resentfully, he could at least pretend that he wasn't relishing every second of the action.

He grinned absently, reaching out to touch her cheek, but kept his eyes on the road. "No heroics," he promised. "When they come *this* way, I'll just wait for them to pass, then we'll go *that way*. There's only one drawback."

"What?" she asked apprehensively.

"It's going to be hell on the paint job."

Her mouth fell open at his philosophical tone, but before she could utter a single, scathing remark, he pointed and said, "Here they come."

The van crept around the blind corner, geared down and started the climb, leaving a trail of thrashing branches in its wake. The Bronco, rumbling impatiently behind the brambles, leaped for the road with a full-throttled roar.

"I'm going to get off the pavement the first chance I get," Adam warned, raising his voice over the sound of the screaming engine, "so—"

"I know, hang on."

Twenty minutes later, after having traveled over every dirt road in the area, Kaylie realized that she wasn't sick anymore. And, although she would have walked over burning coals before admitting it, she could see why some people got hooked on these big cars, or trucks, or whatever they were. Up to now, she had scrupulously avoided riding in anything so big that she had to climb to get into it, but there was something seductive about the amount of power growling beneath the hood— especially when it could be used to escape from a dicey situation.

"Where are we?" She had lost all sense of direction, and neither the state, city, nor county had ventured to put street signs in the back country.

"Beats me. But we're coming back into civilization." He nodded toward the left. "And it won't take long to get oriented."

"You know what I don't understand?" Kaylie said thoughtfully.

"About what?"

"This whole mess. It just doesn't make sense." She sighed with relief as they suddenly rolled onto the smooth asphalt road and lowered the volume of her voice a decibel or two.

"I'll bite. What doesn't?"

"Why these two guys keep coming after me. As far as I can see, it's the height of stupidity. All they had to do was take the goodies from the jewelry store, sell them, then go away and live happily ever after. Instead, they're hanging around, reading newspapers and chasing me—increasing their chances of being caught by about a hundred percent. I ask you, does that make sense?"

Adam checked the speedometer and slowed down to fifty-five. He shook his head, saying, "Not to me. But, right from the start, when they heard that there was even a possibility that you could identify them and they came after you, their intentions were clear. They wanted to get rid of you. They don't intend to leave any witnesses, now or later."

Kaylie shuddered at his matter-of-fact summation.

"But you're right," he went on thoughtfully. "The twenty-thousand-dollar question is, *Why?*."

"You needn't sound so surprised," she mumbled. "I may not have any experience dodging gunmen, but I'm not a dimwit."

"And that's what makes it so interesting. There has to be something pretty big at stake to make them take the extra risk."

Adam wasn't ignoring her so much as pursuing his own train of thought, she realized as she went on. "I'd say that what they got by cleaning out Mr. Jensen constituted a sizable stake."

"Exactly," he said. His look of approval reminded Kaylie of a teacher rewarding a bright student. "And that brings us right back to the beginning of the circle. Why didn't they just disappear with the jewels?"

Kaylie looked out the window at golden fields full of wheat or something that looked like it would end up in a cereal box. They hadn't passed a house in miles, there wasn't a car in sight, and even the rolling hills had been left behind. Well, almost. They were in a picturesque valley dotted with sprawling live oaks, and there was just one long, lazy hill before them.

"Do you suppose we'll ever know?" Her murmured question was rhetorical. She really didn't expect an answer, so she was astonished by his response. Not so much by the words, but by the unrelenting grimness, the absolute conviction of his tone.

"We'll know. Because they'll keep coming after you. And when I stop them, we'll find out."

He glanced obliquely at her, then returned his gaze to the road. Even with her eyes widened in surprise, she was lovely. Probably not in the classical sense, he acknowledged silently, but he had never given a damn about candy box prettiness. She was so incredibly vibrant, so in love with life. She warmed up corners of his soul that he hadn't even known were cold. Her smiling face, her deep blue eyes, the long, slim legs made to wrap around a man and hold him tight, were all his. She was simply and terribly vital to him. To his well-being and his life. And, to keep her safe and near him, he would do whatever he had to do.

A corner of his mouth lifted in a slight, self-mocking smile at the direction his thoughts were taking. Not exactly the stuff lyric poems were made of. Women apparently needed to hear the words when it came to important things, but he didn't imagine Kaylie would be too thrilled with his. He was a simple, direct man, and his words tended to be the same. Hadn't she been telling him that very thing earlier? he thought with a sigh. That he was too terse, too direct? No-frills words from a no-frills man. A man who had just learned with surprise that he was also possessive. Very possessive, when it came to Kaylie West. The thought of another man being the recipient of her smiles, her teasing, her lectures on salesmanship, erased the half smile from his face. No, if there was one thing of which he was certain, it was that when all this was over, he would be the only man who had the right to walk in the bathroom when she was mostly covered with breaking bubbles!

After one quick glance at Adam's face, Kaylie stared through the windshield, looking at the long, gradual climb before them. What had brought that look of grim determination to his face? Well, she acknowledged ruefully, the events of the day were enough to make anyone grim. And she hadn't done much to hold up her end. Looking around when Miss Grace called her name hadn't been one of the smartest things she had ever done. Of course, it *had* given Adam a chance to ride up hill and down dale in his overgrown toy!

Not fair, she chided herself. If it weren't for him, she wouldn't just be the sitting duck he'd talked about, she'd be a dead one. And that would be a serious loss, because lately, since the advent of Adam, life had become very interesting—and confusing. She had spent more hours than she cared to count trying to figure out what made him tick. Unfortunately, she was no nearer the answer now than when she'd started.

He was a complex man. The few years' difference in their ages might as well be light years when it came to experience. She had grown up surrounded by a loving family in a middle-income neighborhood where storming city hall to get a stop sign installed was a big thing. Adam, on the other hand, had dealt with types of scum beyond her imagination. He knew exactly where he was going, while she was content to dally along the way and look around for something interesting. He was serious; she wasn't.

He was also the sexiest man she had ever encountered. And it wasn't just his looks. Sure, broad shoulders, a lean waist, the most fantastic tush she'd ever had the pleasure to watch and long legs were nice. Aside from all that, the man had raw sex appeal dripping from every pore. She knew the second he walked into a room, the exact instant that he turned those hooded, hazel eyes on her. And when he spoke, his words came straight from the shoulder. Dead honest. He would never pretty things up to be kind, never equivocate. She might tease him about that very quality, prod at his massive self-control, but if he ever told a woman that he loved her, she could use that assurance as security at any bank.

"Why do you think they won't give up?" she asked finally, breaking the extended silence.

"They can't afford to. They stuck their necks way out by coming here, and the very fact that we ran told them a lot. What was conjecture on their part before is now a dead certainty. They know for sure that we know who they are."

"Did you get the license number of the van?"

"Um-hmm." Just as they crested the hill, Adam said, "Would you look in the back and see if the map is there? I think we'd better find out exactly where we are."

Kaylie struggled with her seat belt for a moment, then, in exasperation, unclipped it and turned around, kneeling on her seat to look in back. What filled her field of vision was the last thing in the world she expected to see. The black van rolled out from behind a misshapen oak, slid into their lane and came barreling down the road, narrowing the space between them with every second.

"Oh . . . my . . . God."

The undiluted horror in her voice told Adam all he needed to know. Instinctively, he looked up at the rear view mirror. At the same time he grabbed Kaylie's arm and hauled her down into the seat. "Buckle up!" he rapped out. "It's going to be a rough ride."

Kaylie was fumbling with the buckle when the van hit the back of the Bronco. The belt was torn out of her hands, and she raised her arms to protect her face. She fell heavily, almost going to her knees, her forearms cracking against the dashboard. Ignoring the pain that shot up to her elbows, she pushed herself back and groped again for the seat belt.

Adam stomped on the accelerator. He was swearing softly, steadily and inventively. He paused long enough to ask, "Are you all right?"

She nodded, not looking up until the buckle snicked together. "I'm fine. Where are they?"

"Right behind us. But not for long." He gave a grunt of satisfaction as the speedometer needle reached the far right of the gauge and stayed there. Taking another quick glance in the rearview mirror, he said, "That'll give us a little breathing space."

"To do what?"

"A little maneuvering," he said obscurely.

"Just what did they hope to accomplish by that trick?" Kaylie demanded, rubbing some feeling back into her arms.

"To run us off the road and pick us off at their leisure," Adam said flatly.

Kaylie winced at the picture his terse words conjured up. "Oh."

Adam kept his eyes on the terrain ahead, saw something that seemed to please him and eased his foot up on the gas pedal.

"What are you doing?" Kaylie gasped in alarm as the Bronco gradually slowed down.

"Trying to get the upper hand in this little game," he said grimly. He waited patiently for the van to get closer. When it was exactly where he wanted it, he shot off to the right, over the edge of the asphalt and onto an unfenced grassy verge. He kept the steering wheel locked in position so that the Bronco moved in a large circle, similar to a freeway cloverleaf, and arrived back on the road behind the van. The driver of the van had stepped on the brake, but after one look behind him he took off again with the Bronco right on his tail.

Adam took a deep breath and let it out noisily. He flexed his shoulders, the first sign Kaylie had seen of any tension on his part. "If you're taking notes," he said, "remember, it's always better to be the chaser than the chasee."

"What are you going to do?" One glance at his face convinced her that she really didn't want to know.

"Exactly the same thing they were planning."

"I have a better idea. Why don't we turn around and go home?"

"Because they'll turn around, too, and we'll be right back where we started." And with that he stepped on the gas and pointed the screaming Bronco at the van.

Feeling like a passenger in a kamikaze plane, Kaylie stared stoically at the rapidly approaching rear of the van. She blinked in surprise when they passed it. Then, her eyes widened as the Bronco nosed over and nudged the van. It wobbled, then steadied. Once again the Bronco nudged, harder. The van swayed, teetered a bit, then took off down the road. The Bronco kept pace with it, edging in for the kill. This time it didn't nudge, it shoved, using all its considerable muscle. The van wavered, then shot off the side of the road where it dipped into a shallow depression, struggled for a couple of hundred feet to remain upright and finally toppled over on its thunderbolt.

"You did it," Kaylie said faintly.

"Oh, ye of little faith," he murmured, a slight smile relieving his taut features. He slowed the Bronco down and made a U-turn on the empty road.

Looking at him with wide-eyed expectancy, she said, "Now what?"

"I shoot them," he said calmly.

"What?"

His grin was pure male amusement. "Joke, Kaylie. How about tying them up and taking them to the police?"

She looked at him skeptically. "Even *I* know that you just don't walk up to someone and tell them to hold still so you can tie them up. Besides, we don't have any rope. Or maybe you expect them to be unconscious."

"No such luck," he said with a sigh. "Look."

As he drew the Bronco to a stop about fifty feet away, he pointed to the overturned van. The door on the driver's side was slowly being pushed open. The man with sandy hair hauled himself out and dropped to the ground. The dark-haired man followed. He turned and kicked at one of the tires, making no effort to conceal his rage. The two men conferred briefly and turned toward Kaylie and Adam.

"Is this where you go into a karate routine and do something spectacular?" she asked with nervous flippancy.

He shook his head, watching the approaching men through narrowed eyes. Kaylie held her breath, hardly aware of the pulsing mutter of the Bronco's engine, held in check by Adam. The two men came closer, stiff-legged with anger and frustration. The whole scene reminded Kaylie of a bad remake of *Shootout at the OK Corral*. She was about to say so when Adam sighed again.

"Well, damn," he said mildly. "They brought their guns along."

No sooner had he spoken than the two men reached into the waistbands of their jeans. Adam didn't wait to see anything else. He shifted gears, stomped on the gas and pointed the Bronco right at them. The bright sun glinted on steel as guns flew in one direction and men in another. Adam kept going and didn't look back.

After a few minutes he said mildly, "Did you ever find that map?"

"Map? *Map?* That's all you have to say? What about those two back there? Are you just going to leave them?" Kaylie was almost incoherent with adrenaline-induced fury. "Don't you take *anything* seriously?" she asked, supremely unaware of her inconsistency. "They were trying to kill us, and all you did was make jokes!" Her voice cracked on the last word, and she blinked furiously, refusing to shed even one tear in front of the most insensitive man she had ever encountered.

"Bad jokes," he admitted, pulling over to the side of the road and killing the motor. Reaching out and gently rubbing his thumb over her damp lashes, he repeated, "Very bad jokes. I'm sorry, honey, cops have a tendency to do that. It relieves the pressure. Ex-cops have a hard time outgrowing the habit."

He released her seat belt and opened his arms. "Come here for a minute."

She lifted her lashes and eyed him suspiciously. "Why?"

"Because I need a hug."

After a moment's hesitation she flung herself against him and went boneless when his arms closed around her. Her hands laced through his dark hair, cupping his head, bringing his mouth down to hers. Adam's kiss, she thought hazily, was a potent reflection of the man himself. It had the same straight-arrow honesty, the same directness, the same impatience with nonessentials and the same sensuality that turned her bones to jelly.

His tongue touched hers, and she sighed in tacit approval as he deepened the kiss. Blood roared through her veins, warming her entire body, and she stirred restlessly against him, her hands kneading his shoulders in an ageless feminine invitation. He pulled her closer, one hand sliding down to her hips to mold her against him, then, abruptly, he let her go.

He raised his head, sighed sharply, placed his hands on her waist and lifted her back to her seat. Leaning over, he buckled her seat belt and touched her hair in a soft caress. His eyes met hers and saw the bewilderment. He was an idiot, he decided. Of all the places he had available to kiss her, he had to choose a car with bucket seats, in the vicinity of two potential murderers.

"Are you all right?" His hand cupped her cheek, his fingers sliding into the silky seduction of her hair.

Kaylie nodded, promising herself that at another time, in another place, they would pick up where they had left off. But, for now, other things had a higher priority.

"Why didn't you do something with them?" she asked, bypassing tact for forthrightness.

Amusement flickered in his eyes. "Wasn't I heroic enough?"

She waved a hand impatiently, as if swatting away the question. Adam knew exactly what he was; she didn't have to play games to bolster his self-esteem. "I just want to know why you handled things the way you did."

"I'll tell you anything you want to know if you'll answer one question."

"What?" she asked, wondering what she had let herself in for.

"Did you ever find that map?"

With a martyred sigh, she pointed to the floor by his feet. He scooped it up, looked at it for a minute, then set off in the direction in which the Bronco was already pointing.

"I answered your question," she pointed out.

"First of all, I didn't stop and do anything 'spectacular' because I didn't want to put you at risk," he said abruptly.

She looked at him, speechless. He didn't want to put her at risk? What did he call driving like a maniac over roads that would intimidate a mountain goat? What did he call pushing a van off the road with her side of the Bronco? What did he call driving directly at two men with guns? If that wasn't risky, she didn't know the meaning of the word.

"As for the rest of it, all I wanted to do was disable them and get you away. We have the license number of the van, and we can both identify them, so Hodge shouldn't have any trouble picking them up. Hell," he said generously, "I'll even call for a tow truck to go get them."

An hour later he stopped at the small store near his cabin and made the call. When he finished, the plump woman behind the cash register handed him a piece of paper.

"I was going to have my boy take it up later," she explained.

Adam bent his head and read the note. He looked up and met Kaylie's curious gaze. "Telephone message from Hodge," he explained. "He says things are cracking and wants us to come back." Stuffing the note in his pocket, he draped his arm over her shoulders and said, "Let's go break the news to Opal."

"Do you think it's smart to go back?" she asked, remembering the attempted break-in.

"It's past time," he said. "We need to get this mess behind us so we can settle a few other things."

His look, she reflected as she let him lead her back to the Bronco, was both a promise and a threat.

Chapter Nine

"How's Edgar doing?" Kaylie half turned to look at Opal, who was sitting in the back seat of Adam's car, making notes on manuscript pages. The day before, when she and Adam had informed Opal that they would be moving again, her only comment had been, "Good, my regular computer is much better." She had begun packing immediately.

"Hmm?" Opal looked up with a puzzled frown, pushing her reading glasses up to rest on top of her curls.

"Edgar," Kaylie prompted. "What's he up to?"

"He joined the Gray Panthers," Opal said moodily, "and he's pushing for a convention in the Bahamas."

"What does that have to do with your book?"

"Nothing. The man is driving me crazy."

"So you haven't killed him off yet?"

At Adam's question, Kaylie's head turned in his direction. He glanced at the rearview mirror, then obliquely down to meet her eyes. She nodded in answer to his silent question. Yes, she was fine—as long as he was within shouting distance. Yesterday's events were not something she would easily forget. And, if she were fool enough to try, his vigilance was a constant reminder. He hadn't said a word about it, except to tell her that she would be riding back to Saratoga in his car. Then he'd quietly set about checking the alarm system he'd installed in the cabin when it was built. After briefly considering her earlier conclusion about sexy competence, she had felt nothing but relief. Until then, she hadn't thought about the drive back, but she definitely didn't want to be alone in her car.

Opal snorted. "Kill him? The man is worse than Inspector Clouseau."

Adam frowned in thought. "Who?"

"The guy in the Pink Panther movies," Kaylie told him.

"Edgar is so inept, he can hardly tie his shoelaces," Opal stated in exasperation. "Yet every time I set him up, he walks away, leaving someone else to cope with the situation."

"I have a hunch that you like the old guy," Adam said calmly. "I don't think you really want to get rid of him."

Opal snapped her glasses back over her nose, muttered an irritated "Hmmff!" and looked down at the pages in her lap.

Kaylie was still thinking about Adam's alarm system, realizing for the first time how unobtrusive it was. In fact, it was practically invisible. She turned to face him, brushing back the hair that fell over her forehead. "It just dawned on me that I never noticed any of your security devices. I expected your cabin to be bristling with gadgets and things. Either I'm totally unobservant, or else I'm years behind in my ideas. There wasn't even anything different about the doors."

"I don't like extra locks any more than you do," he said blandly.

"So what do you have?"

"Recessed magnetic sensors." At her blank expression, he added, "They're installed in the narrow part of the door, near the bottom. A small magnet closes the circuit on the jamb. Open the door and you break the circuit and trip the alarm. Of course, you don't set them if you're running in and out a lot."

"Of course," she said dryly. "What's to keep someone from taking off the screens?"

"Sensor grids. The only visible sign is a little wired plug."

"What if they break the windows?"

"Shock sensors."

"And they're all small and inconspicuous, right?"

"Right."

"But they're hooked to wires and make a lot of noise if they're set off, right?"

"Right."

"Well, why didn't you tell me that when I was making such a fuss about Opal's house?"

Adam shrugged. "I figured you'd find out soon enough."

Kaylie let out an exasperated sigh. "Adam, that's exactly the kind of thing I was talking about the other day. Benefits, remember? That feature was the benefit you should have pointed out. It would have sold me."

"But you weren't willing to listen," he reminded her.

"You should have been asking me questions," she said briskly. "Now, tell me more about this stuff. What else do you have?"

They were still discussing state of the art security systems and sales techniques when they drove through Saratoga. Adam stopped for a red light, and Kaylie turned to see Mr. Jensen, looking grayer than ever, standing on the corner, waiting to cross the street. She smiled and waved, not sure if he would remember her. Just as the light turned green, his lips twisted in his version of a smile, and he lifted a hand.

Adam turned, pulled up in front of an official building and parked illegally. "Use some of your famous fast talk if they try to give me a ticket," he said to Kaylie, reaching out to touch her hair. "I'll be right back."

She didn't waste his time asking questions; instead, she just leaned back and watched him with enjoyment. It always amazed her how lightly he moved his large body. His stride was long, and his body flowed with the smooth coordination of a man in optimum condition. He also moved fast. He was back with a bulging manila envelope before she had time to do more than wonder whom he was seeing, and why.

A few minutes later Adam eased through the jungle-like entrance of Opal's long driveway. "Watch out for those rocks," he warned the women as they opened their doors and stepped out by an untidy gray heap.

"Richard must be ready to start the stone border in back," Opal said, stepping around the mound.

"Who's Richard?"

"The gardener. He's always got one project or another on tap." Starting up the stairs with her portable computer, she asked, "Does my key still work the lock?"

Adam tucked her printer under one arm and followed her to the door. Shaking the envelope with his free hand, he said, "No, that's what I've got in here. George left everything with Bill Hodge. Let's go in and I'll show you how it all works."

After lunch, Opal went to her office and firmly closed the door.

"I hope all these interruptions haven't thrown her off schedule too much," Kaylie said, looking after her in concern. "Her deadline's getting closer all the time." Automatically, she began stacking the dishes on the table and carrying them to the sink. Adam's hand on hers drew her to a halt.

"I'll help you with those later. Will you come out in back with me for a few minutes?"

She looked up, a grin lighting her face. "Are we going back to the flowers so you can show me how good your memory is? I doubt if Richard put in any roses while we were gone." Her smile faded slowly as she stared up at his face. Not a glimmer of a smile crossed it. "Okay," she said simply, turning toward the door.

He led her to the pepper trees, reached back to pull something from the waistband of his jeans and turned to her with an open palm. "Have you ever used one of these?"

Size doesn't really matter, she reminded herself, swallowing dryly as she looked down. Small guns are just as deadly as large ones. And it was small, not even as big as Adam's hand. Shaking her head, she said, "No."

His voice was matter of fact. "It's time you learned. Come here." When she stood beside him, he said, "I'm taking out the clip so you can get the feel of it without having to worry." He watched through narrowed eyes as she gingerly took the weapon out of his hand.

Kaylie blinked in surprise. "It's heavier than I thought. I don't like this at all," she said for the record, then lifted it tentatively and aimed at a tree trunk. Adam stood quietly, letting her get accustomed to it. "Okay," she said finally. "Now what?"

He pointed to the side of the pistol. "This is the safety. When you flip it forward, the weapon is operable." He waited until she looked up and nodded. "Don't *pull* the trigger, squeeze it." He nodded at a tree and said, "Try it."

She extended her arm, pointed at the tree, closed her eyes, scrunched up her face and squeezed the trigger. Looking up in surprise, she said, "It didn't move."

"Release the safety with your thumb," he said patiently.

"Oh."

"Try it again, and keep your eyes open this time."

Kaylie took imaginary potshots at every bush in the area, following Adam's orders to thumb the safety back, release the safety, aim and shoot. "I'm doing something wrong," she said, frowning in concentration as she aimed the wavering pistol at a big, fat hibiscus. She squeezed the trigger and muttered, "Gotcha! They look different on TV when they do this," she complained, looking over to meet his gaze.

"You're right." He plucked the pistol out of her hand, gripped it in his, raised both arms straight from the shoulder, crossed his thumbs behind the gun butt, covered the fingers of his right hand with those of his left and spread his legs, bending them slightly at the knees. "This is the way they look."

She nodded. "I *knew* something was wrong."

He returned the gun, saying, "Try it. You're going after balance and support, not trying to look graceful on the dueling field."

Kaylie copied his stance, muttering, "I feel silly."

"Feel as silly as you want, it's better than being dead." He eyed her critically, then rearranged her fingers. "Put your feet a little further apart, and don't bend your knees quite so much. Pretend you're skiing. That's better," he said approvingly as she adjusted her position. "Okay, come over here by me, aim at that tree," he pointed to one with a thick trunk, "and see if you feel steadier."

She moved forward, bent her knees, raised both hands and pointed the gun at the tree. Her brows rose in surprise. "Quite a difference," she admitted.

"Good, you're a natural," he said, reaching out to lace his fingers in her hair, his palm cupping her cheek. She *was* good. But there was a hell of a difference between playacting and the real thing, he worried. And even a bigger one between trees and a living target.

Kaylie was obviously having doubts of her own. "I'm not too sure about this, Adam. I've done it all without any bullets. How do I know I could hit anything if I had to?"

Good question, he brooded. "This is a crash course, honey. If push comes to shove, your target will be close enough and big enough to hit." He managed to keep his tone more reassuring than he felt.

She checked the safety and returned the gun to him with finality. "I don't know if I could aim this at someone and pull the trigger."

"Even if your life depended on it?" he asked roughly.

She thought about it. "I don't know. Do you think there's a chance that I might find out?"

"I don't know," he said, repeating her earlier words, hating the look of anxiety clouding her eyes. Replacing the clip and holstering the pistol, he added in a lighter tone, "Let's just call this a lesson in prevention. If you just remember to release the safety and squeeze, you'll be fine." He hoped. He draped his arm over her shoulders and turned toward the house. "Let's go get those dishes done."

Adam stood in the living room doorway, looking down at Kaylie. She was lying on her side on a bright, oval rag rug in the center of the floor, with her back to him, her head propped up by a bent arm, reading a book. She had changed into her hip-hugging red shorts and a matching knit shirt. Her left leg rose slowly and rhythmically to an impossible angle, lowered to the floor, then repeated the process. Whatever she was doing, he decided with a small grin, he wasn't about to stop her. The lifting action of her long, slim leg tightened the shorts over the sweet flare of her bottom. He crossed his arms over his chest and leaned a shoulder against the jamb.

Kaylie rolled over, bringing the book along, and started to work on her right leg. Her gaze settled on a pair of dark running shoes in the doorway. It moved up past jeans, a brown leather belt, a blue chambray shirt stretched to capacity over a broad chest, then stopped when it reached the intrigued expression on Adam's face.

She blinked. "What are you doing?"

Pushing himself away from the door and coming to a stop directly beside her, he said, "Watching you. What are *you* doing?"

"Killing two birds with one stone." Tucking the book between her body and the floor, she explained, "I hate to exercise, so I read while I work on my hips and thighs."

Slowly he walked around her, finally coming to a stop behind her. "What's the matter with them?" he finally asked as he lay down, his thigh nudging the small of her back as he shifted his weight.

"Not too much now," she said, wondering why he was behind her, what he was doing and determined that she wouldn't turn around and look. "But they're a bit like Edgar. If I don't keep on top of them, they get out of control." Despite her resolution, when his body heat merged with hers, she looked up over her shoulder and found him closer than she'd expected. He was sprawled behind her, his arms folded as they had been when he stood in the doorway, but instead of resting on his chest, they were resting on her hip, his chin resting on his hands. With his chest pressed against her back, she felt as if she had just been surrounded.

He nudged the book beneath her shoulder with his knee. "What are you reading?"

"Just a little thing I found called *The Art of Gentle Persuasion*," she lied. "It's subtitle is *How to Make a Hard-headed Man Recognize His Sales Potential*."

"I thought that was the one you were going to write."

"I changed my mind," she told him, pressing down on her arm to keep the book where it was. It was a losing battle, she learned, as he kept exerting pressure against it with his knee. Inevitably, as the book moved forward on the rug, her shoulder slid along with it until she landed on her back with her head resting on Adam's knee.

Adam considered the cover of the book with a speculative gaze. Two men, each dressed in a *gi*, the traditional karate costume, were trying to kick the daylights out of each other. "Brushing up on your martial arts a little?"

"No such thing," she said stoutly, pushing the damning book across the rug.

"Planning to dump me again?" he asked, humor lighting his eyes.

"I don't need a book for that," she answered, her brows lifting loftily. "I can handle you."

Adam grinned, and Kaylie suddenly felt like a mouse caught between the paws of a large, indulgent, golden-eyed cat.

"Can you, now?" he murmured.

"Um-hmm." An answering smile of pure bravado curved her lips, but she lowered her lids to avoid meeting the challenge gleaming behind his dark lashes.

Too late, she remembered his knack of turning the slightest weakness to his advantage. A rustle and a loss of warmth were her only warnings. The knee she was using as a pillow disappeared, and when she opened her eyes he was looking down at her, his breath warming her lips. Her lashes lowered again as he bent his head. His kiss was a warm, encompassing declaration. His lips settled on hers possessively, and his tongue seemed to draw sweetness and strength from the center of her body.

Adam lifted his head and looked down at her. An element of savage, triumphant, utterly male satisfaction flickered in his eyes at the sight of her dazed expression. She shifted restlessly, her fingers involved in tactile exploration. They slid up his arms, savored the texture of crisp, dark hair, moved over the soft material of his shirt to his shoulders and settled at his nape. He obeyed the slight tug, touching his lips to the corner of her mouth, to her jaw, and stringing a line of kisses down to her chin.

Trapping her restless legs with one muscular, denim-covered thigh, he slid his hand beneath her shoulders and cupped her head, his arm lifting her, bringing the tips of her breasts against the warmth of his chest.

Kaylie felt every move he made, knew exactly what he was doing, but was stunned by the gentle assault. Adam, she thought hazily, was a deceptive man. He emanated strength and a sense of massive restraint, and those very qualities induced in her a vast feeling of security. On one level—that of an individual relying on him for protection—her instincts were utterly sound, she knew. It was on another level—that of female to his male—that the whole thing broke down. Once she crossed some invisible line, he became a hunter, a pirate committed to victory and spoils. And right now, she thought, a tremor running through her, she was the prize he was after.

She shivered again as the tip of his tongue seared a path along the neckline of her knit top, dipping down from one shoulder, hesitating briefly to savor the soft flesh above her breasts, and slanting back up the other side. If this was what she got for telling him that she could handle him, she thought, then obviously she'd just have to do it more often!

Adam, about to cover her lips with his, stopped to watch an utterly feminine, thoroughly intriguing smile tilt the corners of her mouth. "Am I amusing you?" he murmured.

Kaylie tilted her head thoughtfully, blue eyes gleaming through long brown lashes. "Distracting might be a better word," she hedged, avoiding the more appropriate ones like arousing, stimulating and seducing. If the complacent look in his eyes was any indication, she thought, drawing a ragged breath, her honest response had already given more away than she liked. These skirmishes were enjoyable, but it was a bit too early in their relationship to even consider surrender.

Adam slid his arm out from under her. Shifting until he lay beside her, his head propped on one bent arm, he traced a finger down the still damp path his tongue had taken. He stopped at the soft, shadowy cleft between her breasts. When her eyes widened, he asked, "Have you ever thought about living in San Diego?"

Kaylie swallowed dryly, staring up at him with round eyes. Their relationship was growing by quantum leaps! "What does San Diego have to offer that I can't get in San Francisco?" she whispered.

"Me."

And that simple statement ended the conversation— at least as far as Adam was concerned. For Kaylie, it wasn't so easy. Give up her apartment? Her friends? Her business contacts? For what? But before any further questions bombarded her, before any answers appeared, Adam kissed her. Every inch of Adam kissed her. His warm hand worked its way beneath her shirt, settling in the center of her back and urging her body closer, until she was resting against him, from her bare toes to her head tucked in the curve of his arm.

"Adam?" Kaylie didn't know if seconds or minutes had passed when she put the heel of her hand on his shoulder and pushed. When her tentative gesture had no effect, she put more muscle behind it. "Adam, please."

Every inch of her body felt his tension, the sheer male hunger he made no attempt to conceal. The reluctance with which he loosened his hold on her, the unsatisfied desire that still claimed him when he raised his head, plus the look of taut expression on his face, told her in no uncertain terms that his massive control was about to crack. His sharply exhaled sigh only served to emphasize the point.

"What?"

The word seemed to come out through gritted teeth, and Kaylie groaned silently. This probably wasn't the time to conduct a meaningful conversation regarding their relationship.

"What?" he repeated, raising himself up on one elbow and looking down at her.

"It's just that things have been happening so fast," she began tentatively. "I mean, this situation isn't at all normal, and . . ." Her words faded away as she forced her gaze from his third shirt button to his face.

"And what?" he asked unencouragingly.

"I just think we need to talk," she ended with a rush.

"Talk," he repeated grimly. With another sharply exhaled breath, he rolled over on his back, hauling her along with him.

"Woman, you sure do pick your times. What do you want to talk about?"

"Edgar," Opal said, coming around the corner from the hall. Her tone was as grim as Adam's. "I'm glad I caught you at a good time." Dropping down into a chair, she took off her glasses and stared out the window.

Kaylie jerked in surprise and tried to move away, but Adam wrapped his arm around her waist, stopping her. He pulled a pillow down from the sofa for their heads, and within seconds they were on their sides, Kaylie tucked spoon-fashion in front of him, looking up at Opal.

"What's he done now?" Adam asked in resignation, his thumb coming to rest just beneath Kaylie's breast.

"I bought him one of those gadgets that makes malts for his birthday, so he could make those disgusting protein and papaya drinks he favors," Opal said broodingly. "I thought I could squeeze some juice from a poinsettia stalk into it someday. Just to have another option, you know?" She looked down at the two on the floor and waited for their nods.

"But I still had one oleander trick up my sleeve. There's nothing he enjoys more in the evening than reading, with a fire crackling in the fireplace. So I stacked up some dried oleander branches on the hearth and clogged up part of the flue. All the man had to do," she said aggrievedly, "was sit still, burn the blasted things and breathe the fumes."

"But he didn't?" Kaylie ventured in a quivering voice, trying to move away from Adam's questing thumb.

Opal shook her head, a wrathful gleam in her eye. "He threw a party instead. Hordes of people came and opened up the windows to get some air circulating."

"What happened?" Adam asked, intrigued in spite of himself.

"Edgar spent his time in the kitchen making those revolting drinks, and several perfectly innocent people broke out in a rash."

"So what's he doing now?"

"Training for a marathon," Opal said gloomily, staring out the window in silence. Several minutes passed before her head tilted thoughtfully. Her eyes narrowed, and her fingers drummed absently on the arm of the chair. "Ha!" she exclaimed, getting out of the chair and moving toward the hall. Seconds later, her office door slammed.

Kaylie flipped on the light switch in the hall and walked down to Opal's office. Knocking on the door, she called, "Opal?" After waiting and hearing nothing but a disinterested mumble, she opened the door, stopped as a nasty word was directed, presumably, at the word processor, and peeked in. "Opal? Mr. Jensen is here to see you."

O .P. Shriver turned around and looked at her. "What?"

Kaylie blinked, waiting for her godmother's personality to emerge. "Mr. Jensen's out in the living room with Adam."

"Oh. I'll come right out. Let me save this stuff first." Opal poked a button, waited for the machine to buzz and click, then got up.

"I didn't know you knew him socially."

"Leon? We've been friends for years. He drops by every now and then. He's lonely, poor man. His wife has been in a convalescent hospital for several months."

The two men were sitting quietly, apparently having used up their supply of small talk, and they looked up in relief when Kaylie and Opal walked into the living room. The night air had grown cool, and Adam got up to close the windows.

"Leon! How are you?" Opal hugged the older man, then stepped back to eye him critically. "Not so good, I'd say. How's Mary?"

"About the same," Mr. Jensen said with a tired smile. "I just thought I'd stop by for a few minutes."

Opal tucked her arm through his. "Come out in the kitchen, and I'll make some tea. You can tell me all about the robbery. You *were* covered by insurance, weren't you?"

Adam rummaged in the closet and pulled out two dark sweaters that matched their jeans. Tossing one to Kaylie, he said, "Do you want to go for a walk? I could use some exercise."

She nodded amiably, pulling the sweater over her head. "We're going to disappear as soon as we get outside," she commented lightly, wishing that Adam hadn't made such a point of asking her to change into dark clothing after dinner. He was, she'd learned, a man who calmly prepared for all eventualities—even a walk in the dark—and she was a nervous woman who would cheerfully wait in a locked room until the good guys caught the bad ones.

"That's the whole point." Adam stopped briefly at the panel in the hallway and poked some buttons. He put on the sweater, turned off the hall light and opened the door.

"When did you start wearing a beeper?" Kaylie asked, pointing at a small, rectangular device attached to his belt.

"Since George left me one. He added a few refinements of his own on the outside perimeters. If anyone comes through the gate or the shrubbery, I'll know it." Adam took her hand and led her around the house to the back yard.

"Terrific," Kaylie said, clenching her jaw to stop her teeth from chattering. "Where are Bill Hodge and his merry men? Why aren't they out here patrolling the place? Why did he call us back and then just ignore us?"

"I talked to him a while ago. He sent someone out to pick up our two friends, and he's waiting for them to get back. He's right where he should be, and I'm here," Adam said firmly.

Never fear, Adam's here? Kaylie wondered in agitation, then knew it was the simple truth. He had proven that yesterday. And now, here, in the dark, he was still in his element. He moved like a creature of the night, without a sound. And he was a patient man. He was waiting to finish the afternoon's conversation that had been aborted when Opal walked in, and he would wait with the same unflappable composure for the evening's events to unfold.

It wasn't fair, she thought, feeling the tension coiling through her body. She didn't even know for sure that there was anything to worry about, and she was a basket case. Adam was simply unnatural. He had no nerves. He had probably been born with an excess of hormones or something. Definitely hormones, she thought with a sudden grin, remembering his reaction that afternoon.

"Tell me more about your beeper," she demanded suddenly.

"First of all," he said lazily, "it doesn't beep. It's color coded."

"I was afraid you'd say something like that."

"Why?"

"Because," she said, staring at it with morbid fascination, "it's glowing!"

Chapter Ten

Adam swore. The one word, earthy and succinct, aptly summed up his self-disgust. What the hell was he doing allowing himself to be distracted at a time like this? It didn't matter that it was Kaylie who was doing the distracting—her presence had been an occupational hazard since the day he'd met her, and he should have known better. He was supposed to be protecting her, for God's sake, not hanging over her like some hormone-ridden teenager.

He pressed a button on the small case and watched as an amber light flickered. "Come on." He grabbed her hand and ran back the way they had just come. "They're out in front."

Since she had no other choice, she followed him. "How do you know it's them? Maybe it's a dog, or a cat," she whispered hopefully.

"Animals are too small; they wouldn't set off the alarm. And I'm not sure that it's them," he said softly, stopping as they reached the corner of the house. "But until I find out differently, I'm assuming it is. Be quiet now," he warned, releasing her hand. "Stay right behind me."

The moon was high above, weaving between some clouds, and a pale, silvery light worked its way through the leafy trees, leaving the yard in dappled shadows. Kaylie squinted, peering into the farthest corners, trying to adjust her eyes to the darkness. They had been standing in a cleared area in the back, and it had been almost light enough to read a book. She closed her eyes for a moment, took a deliberate breath and slowly exhaled. Her blood was making such an uproar racing through her veins that she wouldn't have been surprised if the noise it made set off another alarm.

Adam had turned into a statue; she couldn't even hear him breathing. But, looking up, she saw that he was very much alive. His eyes were fixed on the yard, his gaze methodically covering it, almost inch by inch. And that took a lot of doing, Kaylie thought, considering how large it actually was. Opal's property covered about three sloping, graded acres, with the house dropped on a flat spot roughly in the middle. That left a lot of yard, none of it neatly manicured, and a lot of hiding places for people who wanted to remain unseen.

After enduring several minutes of silence, Kaylie was exhausted from the effort of listening and watching. Especially when there was nothing to hear and even less to see. She was about to say as much to Adam, when his hand clamped over her mouth.

"Not a word," he breathed in a voice so soft she barely heard it, and he kept his hand where it was until she nodded. "I don't want you trapped in the house if those two have managed to get this far, so we're heading for the shadowed area in front."

She nodded again and reached out to touch his arm. Just as her fingers brushed the soft, nubby sweater, a branch snapped. It wasn't close, she realized, probably near the street, but accustomed as she now was to the taut stillness, it came with all the impact of a gunshot. Her startled gasp was muffled as Adam's hand once again covered her lips.

"Ready?" he murmured, slowly dropping his hand and reaching for hers.

She squeezed his fingers and moved closer. Adam glanced up at the moon, waited patiently until it slid behind a cloud, then grasped her wrist and moved. They glided around the corner of the house, bypassing the stairs to the porch because the light from the windows illuminated it like a stage. After stepping carefully over a few loose rocks by the passenger side of his car, they stopped on the other side beneath a huge carob tree.

Adam tugged her back against the tree trunk, deep in the shadows. "Stay right here," he ordered, the softness of his voice in no way diminishing the authority behind his words. "I don't want you to move a muscle while I'm gone, understand?"

"Where are you going?" Kaylie looked up, trying to see his face in the deep shadow, and saw without surprise that her relaxed companion of the past couple of weeks was gone. The man who faced her had been molded in other spheres, places with wars and street gangs. He knew exactly what he was doing, and all he required from her was obedience.

He nodded toward the street. "Out there to see what's going on. Here, I want you to take this, just in case."

Kaylie knew what was coming even before her fingers touched the cold metal. She shook her head violently. "You might need it."

"Damn it, Kaylie," he muttered impatiently. "I can take care of myself. I'll call out when I come back, but if anyone else gets here first, shoot."

A branch moved noisily by the entrance to the driveway, followed by a muffled curse. Adam shifted his weight like a great cat.

"And remember to release the blasted safety." His hand touched the top of her head in a brief caress, and then he was gone. He took two flowing, silent steps and disappeared into the shadows. Even though she knew in which direction he was heading, she couldn't find him. Nothing moved, not a branch, not a leaf, and especially not a broad-shouldered, slim-hipped man who carried her heart in his two large hands.

If anyone else gets here first, shoot. Kaylie gingerly eased the gun down on the car, careful not to let metal clang against metal, and considered Adam's words. Could she do it? She wished she knew. Leaning back against the rough tree bark, becoming part of the silent night, she visualized scenes in which she was required to shoot the lethal weapon lying on the fender beside her. If Adam were in a life and death fight and his opponent had the advantage, what would she do? Definitely use the gun. But what if she shot Adam? Maybe shooting over their heads would be better, she hedged.

What if that someone had a gun or a knife and caught Adam by surprise? And suppose the attacker was far enough away that she had a clear shot at him? Kaylie's answer came so quickly that it should have surprised her, but it didn't. She would do her best to shoot him. Adam—and God only knew when it had happened, because she certainly didn't—was a part of her, and no one could be allowed to harm him.

But when he'd left her, Adam's concern had been for *her* safety. In fact, she acknowledged with a wry smile, he would be astonished to hear that she had ever contemplated having to come to his aid. No, he had left the weapon with her for one purpose only—to protect herself. All she had to do was release the safety, aim and squeeze. Could she do it? She hoped so.

A soft sound near the driveway broke the silence. Her head snapped up, and she peered through the mosaic of light and shadow, the sound of her thudding heart loud in her ears. It wasn't Adam, she knew with certainty. He might be out there treading on the same mat of fallen pine needles and leaves, but he would be lethally silent.

With a suddenness that was shocking, a man stepped out from the darkness about fifty feet away into an open patch of pale moonlight. He trod cautiously over the sloping ground as he eyed the darkness ahead, his right hand slightly extended and curiously still. A sense of fatalistic calm, almost relief that now everything was in the open, settled over Kaylie as she recognized him. So Bill Hodge's men had missed them, and now it was up to Adam, she thought with a curious lack of fear.

Rebellion poured through her at the thought, warming her cold fingers. It wasn't Adam's responsibility, it was *theirs*. They were a team, whether he knew it or not, and she wouldn't sit meekly on the sidelines waiting for two armed men to descend on him.

Ignoring Adam's orders to stay put and timing her movements to those of the man in the clearing, Kaylie edged around the hood of the car to keep him in sight. Her heart leaped when he spun around to face the fringe of darkness behind him, aiming a wavering gun. Even though his back was to her, she knew by his jerky movement that he was on edge, jumping at real or imagined sounds. She took another step forward, careful not to disturb the pile of rocks at her feet.

Billy, or his friend, whichever one it was, had just about reached the end of his rope, she realized. Whether or not he knew that Adam was playing cat to his mouse, he was rattled. Then, instinctively, she knew it had to be the high-strung Billy; his partner, the soft-spoken one, was less likely to panic and probably the more dangerous of the two. But the way Billy was swinging his pistol around, he was a menace to anyone in sight, including himself.

Out of the corner of her eye, almost directly in line with the muzzle of Billy's gun, Kaylie saw a slight shift in the shadows and knew it was Adam. She had no doubts; she *knew* he was there, waiting with the patience of a stalking cat for the right moment. She moved back a fraction, and her foot brushed a rounded stone. She came to a dead stop. She could give Adam the chance he needed, she realized with a sudden lift.

Bending over, she hefted several of the rocks, selecting those that fit comfortably in her hand. She lobbed the first one well over Billy's head. As it fell with a thud to the ground behind him, he whirled around, waving the gun in a half circle. While he was still off balance, she threw a second one. That one went like a missile and landed right between his shoulders. It was pretty ragged, she decided critically, but still effective. It didn't hit his right shoulder, but at least he dropped his gun.

There was no need for a third. Adam erupted out of the dark and was all over him like a swarm of bees.

Deciding that discretion was the better part of valor, and that when Adam came back she'd better be where he'd stashed her, she turned away with a satisfied smirk. Did she ever hit anything, indeed! Maybe now he'd take back that patronizing offer to win a teddy bear for her. On the other hand, considering that she hadn't hit what she'd aimed for, some practice was definitely in order before they went to the fair. Moving back to the other side of the car, flushed with success, she wondered belatedly about Billy's partner, the quiet one.

As if her thoughts had conjured him up, he stepped into sight, about twenty feet away, saying softly, "That's quite a throwing arm you have. You hit Billy a good one."

Kaylie swallowed dryly. "Baseball," she uttered foolishly.

Sauntering a few feet closer, he said in a gently reproving tone, "Lady, you've been giving me and old Billy a lot of grief."

"Then you shouldn't go around robbing stores and scaring people half to death," she said, lulled by his reasonable tone.

"We didn't have much choice. We needed the money."

"Some people actually work to get what they want," she pointed out in what she hoped was a calm, sensible voice.

"Oh, we've worked, me and Billy. Worked real hard. This time around, though, we needed a lot of cash, fast."

"Why?" she asked with genuine curiosity.

He stopped about ten feet away, shoving his hands in his back pockets. "You sure do ask a lot of questions."

"Why are you answering them?" she asked, knowing in advance that she wasn't going to like the answer.

"Because you won't be spreading the word around, and I got a few minutes to kill until Billy takes care of your friend."

This is insane, Kaylie thought. She was standing here making polite conversation while across the yard two men were, except for an occasional grunt, silently trying to knock each other's brains out. Although he hadn't made one threatening gesture, she backed away from the man before her, up against the car, spreading her hand along the fender. Her whole body jerked when her fingers touched the cold metal of the weapon Adam had left for her.

If anyone else gets here first, shoot.

Her hand closed over the gun, and she slid to the right until she stood in front of it. "My, uh, friend is pretty good," she said matter-of-factly, lifting the pistol and slowly sliding it into the waistband of her jeans. It was cold against her back and took up every spare centimeter of space. "What makes you think Billy can take him?"

"He's a mean one," he said proudly. "Fights real dirty. Never saw him whipped yet."

Kaylie took a ragged breath, hoping that Adam was showing Billy a few nasty tricks of his own. "So why did you need the money?" she asked again. If she could keep him talking until Adam showed up, and if he didn't get any more hostile than he already was, she just might get through the evening without shooting someone.

"For an investment."

She stared at him as he smiled and teetered back on his heels. "You play the stock market?" she asked politely.

"Real estate."

"You guys want to be landlords?" she asked in confusion.

"We want to be *someone*," he said, the grin leaving his face, "and this is our chance. And no one—not you, not your friend, not anyone—is going to stop us."

"Well, why did you have to rob poor Mr. Jensen's jewelry store to be someone?" she burst out. "Why didn't you go to the bank and borrow money the way other people do?"

His short laugh was not amused. "We're not exactly good credit risks. Neither is our partner."

Partner? This thing was getting more complicated by the minute. "You mean there's someone else mixed up in the robbery?"

"Yeah, but he's been nothing but a pain in the, uh, bad news, since we did it."

One part of her mind considered the man's contradictory behavior. He obviously planned to kill her, yet he wouldn't swear in front of her. The rest of her was occupied with what he was telling her. A third man. What did he have to do with it? Were the police aware of his existence?

"It looks to me like you and Billy took all the risks," she said. "How did someone else get involved?"

"It was his idea. He was the one who knew that a consortium was considering a chunk of real estate just outside town for a convention center. It's going to have hotels, a mall, the works. If we have the right kind of money, we can get in on the ground floor. In a year or two we'll be millionaires."

Aware that the sounds of struggle had ceased, Kaylie rushed to the next question. "Then what? Once you have all the money you want? Travel around the world, find a tropical paradise?"

"Hell no. Billy and me, we're ready to settle down. Here. We'll get married, raise families, be pillars of society. Yeah," he said, nodding, "our kids will go to school here. We'll donate money to hospitals, make speeches, and maybe someday I'll run for mayor. So you can see," he said reasonably, "what kind of trouble you'd cause. If you're as good as they said in the paper, you could come back to visit the old lady, run into one of us in town and blow the whole thing sky high."

"But I'm not," she told him, lying without a qualm. "The article in the paper was all wrong."

"Not according to your friend the professor," he said flatly.

Kaylie looked at him in disbelief. "Professor Wyckoff?"

He nodded. "Yep. Our partner called him. Know what he said?"

She shook her head, groaning silently. The good professor was not modest about what she had learned under his tutelage.

"That you're *better* than what they said. And if it would help, he'd come and swear under oath that you're capable and qualified to identify our voices." He sounded as if he had quoted the line a number of times. "And that's why me and Billy and poor old Mr. Jensen can't afford to have you running around loose." He watched with a humorless smile as she absorbed his words.

"Mr. Jensen?" she asked in astonishment.

He nodded. "He's the one who came up with the deal. Said we could sell the jewels, and with the insurance money, we'll come pretty close to having what we need."

She felt a wrench of sadness at the thought of the worn, gray man sitting in the kitchen with Opal. What had driven him to dealing with the likes of these two? His wife's illness? Had despair caused him to consider such an alliance? Her empathy was overcome by a more immediate surge of fear when the man before her withdrew his hands from his pockets. His right hand held something dark, and with a snick, a long blade shot out, glittering wickedly in the pale light.

"Billy seems to be done with your friend," he said calmly, stepping toward her. "I guess it's time for me to get to work. I can't expect him to do everything."

"I've got a gun," she told him shakily.

He stopped, his gaze speculative. Shaking his head, he said, "I don't believe you." And he came another step closer.

"I do," she insisted, reaching behind her and pulling it out. "See?"

He stopped again, disgustedly shaking his head, as if wondering what fool had allowed her to walk around with a loaded weapon. "So you do," he said finally. "But you know what, sugar face? I don't think you're going to use it." And he eased forward another step.

"I don't want to," she said honestly. "But I will, if you come any closer."

His sudden grin was the first genuine emotion that Kaylie had seen him exhibit. "I got a better idea. How would you like to marry me and join me in my life of crime?" he asked.

"No, thank you," she said politely. "I have this friend, the one who's taking care of Billy, remember? I don't think he'd like it. No, don't come any closer! I meant what I said." He was getting uncomfortably close, she thought nervously. Where in the ever-loving world was Adam?

"Are you much of a gambler?" he asked suddenly.

"No." She watched through narrowed eyes as he came another step closer.

"Well, I am, sugar face, and I'm betting that you're not going to use that gun on me." Before the last word was out of his mouth he rushed at her.

Forgetting everything that Adam had taught her, Kaylie acted instinctively. She ran, literally, for her life. Around the car and right to the porch, where the moonlight illuminated the entire area. She raced up the stairs, only to be stopped by the screen door that Adam had somehow secured behind them. Turning, she leaned against the door frame and clasped the pistol with both hands the way he had shown her.

"Stop!" she said fiercely. "Don't make me do it." She looked down at an expressionless face. Icy gray eyes stared back at her, eyes that gave no quarter.

"Sugar face," he said deliberately, his soft voice ruffling her nerve endings, "you can't." And he put his foot on the bottom step.

"Dear God," she whispered, watching as he moved to the next one, "you're right. I can't."

Adam's voice broke the charged silence. "Don't worry, Kaylie. I can."

Her gaze shifted to him, and she didn't doubt him for a second. Neither did the man at the bottom of the stairs. He slowly dropped his knife and raised his hands. Kaylie didn't blame him. Adam looked as dangerous as a bomb about to explode.

Bill Hodge appeared out of the shadows, took one look at the charged scene and said briskly, "I'll take over, Adam."

Adam, his eyes narrowed in fury, kept his eyes on the man standing so close to Kaylie.

"Give me the gun," Hodge said sharply, after a quick look at Adam's face.

Kaylie hadn't realized that she was holding her breath until the swirling rage began to fade from Adam's eyes, and he silently handed over Billy's gun.

"What are you doing here?" she asked Hodge, sighing in relief.

He grinned. "I got a call from Opal. She said Mr. Jensen was here and wanted to give us some interesting information about the robbery. Looks like we got more than we bargained for." He gestured to someone, and another man joined the group.

"There's someone over there on the grass," the newcomer said with a peculiar expression, glancing obliquely at Adam.

With a shrug, Adam said, "He was after Kaylie. I got to him first."

"Now, Adam, really," Kaylie said several hours later in a reasonable tone. "How do you expect me to shoot someone who calls me sugar face?" She grinned as he gagged.

She was sitting on the couch, feet propped on the coffee table, and Adam was right next to her. He hadn't been more than a few inches away from her ever since they had all trooped into the house. Hodge, his men, the robbers and Mr. Jensen were finally gone.

"What do you think will happen to him?"

"Jensen?"

She nodded.

"Probably not too much. The insurance company hasn't paid him yet, and it was his own store he was trying to steal from. And he did turn state's evidence on his partners. I think he'll be okay. But the other two are a different story. They have records a mile long. They should be out of circulation for some time."

He didn't sound a bit sorry, Kaylie thought. She sighed and leaned back on the couch. The explanations had gone on forever, but nothing much had been added to the version she'd heard in the yard. It had begun with Mr. Jensen's desperation and his introduction to the Texans. After the robbery, when Kaylie became a source of danger, Leon Jensen realized that he'd lost control of the situation. It soon became obvious that the only way he could avoid becoming an accessory to murder was to turn himself in and take them down with him.

Adam slid an arm behind Kaylie, sighing when she rested her head on his shoulder. "My God," he sighed. "Are we really alone?"

She nodded.

"Where's Opal?" he demanded, looking around as if he expected her to crawl out from under the couch.

"In bed."

Rolling several strands of her silky hair between his fingers, he said abruptly, "It's going to be a long time before I forget the sight of you standing on the stairs pointing that gun. Why didn't you stay where I told you to?"

"I thought you could use some help." Ignoring his disgusted mutter, she said, "And I did help. Admit it."

"Okay, so I got to him faster with your help, but look what happened then. You ended up standing under a spotlight, waving a gun—"

"I held it just the way you showed me," she interrupted.

"—and telling the guy you couldn't shoot him." Before she could do more than open her mouth in protest, he abruptly changed the subject. "What did you want to talk about this afternoon?"

Tactful as ever, she thought in resignation. With all the subtlety of a steamroller. Well, she wasn't about to haul the question of their relationship kicking and screaming into the conversation, so he'd just have to settle for the next item on the agenda.

"Work," she said brightly, and was pleased with his disgruntled expression.

"Oh."

"You know I've been thinking of starting my own business, don't you?"

"Um-hmm."

"Well, I've had another idea."

"You're not going to train people for sales work?"

"After trying my techniques on you for a week, I've decided that there has to be an easier way to make a buck. How would you like a business partner?"

"I've got one," he reminded her, before he remembered that he was trying to get her to San Diego.

"Another one," she said patiently. "George can make the widgets, you can tell people what kind and how many they need, and I'll sell them. How does that sound?"

"Fine." He didn't give a damn what she did as long as she did it near him.

"I've got the money to buy into the business," she told him.

"You don't have to do that."

"Yes, I do," she said firmly. "I don't want to work *for* you, Adam. You'd be an awful boss. I want to work *with* you."

"Think I'll be any better as a partner?" he asked with a grin.

She sighed. "Probably not. But *I'd* have more leverage as a partner."

He shifted restlessly. "I'll talk to George."

"You do that," Kaylie said affably.

"Earlier this afternoon, when I mentioned San Diego," he said abruptly, "I wasn't talking about work."

Her brows shot up in mock surprise. "Really?"

"Really," he said, resisting an urge to strangle her—or kiss her silly.

"What were you talking about?"

"Us. Being together."

Her heart leaped. "How?" she asked cautiously, looking him straight in the eye.

"How the hell do you think!" he said with a scowl. "In a house!"

"Adam," she said, patting his thigh to cushion the blow, "I don't know how to break this to you, but I don't make a habit of living with men."

He captured her hand, keeping it in place with one of his. "I'm not talking about men," he said irritably. "I'm talking about me. I want you in my house, taking bubble baths in my tub, and sleeping bare-bottomed in my bed."

"For how long?" she asked carefully, wondering if he was just hesitant about using the words she needed to hear, or if he wasn't thinking of permanent ties. "Are we talking about a weekend, or a temporary arrangement of some kind?"

He looked down at her anxious face and felt his heart turn over. "We're talking about every day for the next fifty or sixty years and whatever comes after that.

Marriage, kids, grandkids, the whole works, Kaylie. I want it all; with you.''

He stared at her, waiting for her answer. But the voice he heard came from behind him.

''Ah, you're still up,'' Opal said in pleased surprise. ''Good.'' She dropped down into the chair across from them, a fuzzy bathrobe wrapped around her. ''I decided to let Edgar live,'' she said abruptly.

Adam's arm tightened around Kaylie in frustration.

''He must be relieved,'' she said shakily.

''He doesn't know yet,'' Opal muttered.

They waited patiently.

''He had to have his stomach pumped.''

Hazel and blue eyes stared at her accusingly.

''*I* didn't do it,'' she said defensively.

''Who else is there?'' Adam asked.

''I don't know,'' she said grimly, getting up and heading for her office. ''But I'll find out.''

Adam's gaze pinned Kaylie down. ''Don't you owe me an answer?''

She nodded. ''Yes.''

''Well?''

Blue eyes laughed up at him. ''Yes.''

''Yes?''

''*Yes!*''

Epilogue

Kaylie stretched and trailed her fingers down Adam's bare back. They meandered down an equally bare hip and thigh before he turned his head on the pillow and slanted a grin down at her.

"You looking for trouble, lady?"

"Would it do me any good?" she asked hopefully.

He tugged her into his arms. "Nope. Not for another week, or until the doctor says so, then I'll give you all you can handle."

She rubbed her cheek on the crisp hair matting his chest. "We don't have to tell her," she tempted in her best come-hither drawl.

"We can wait. We've got all the time in the world."

Kaylie sighed. She was well acquainted with that voice. After three years of marriage, she knew when she could wrap Adam Masters around her little finger—and that was most of the time. Of course, he could do the same to her, so there wasn't much of an advantage there. But all bets were off when circumstances affected her safety or well-being. And this—at least in his opinion—was one of those times.

He had gone with her to the six-week childbirth class, and when the time came, coached her through the long hours of the night. When it was over, she held the baby, and he held them both, his tears burning into her hair. And for the last five weeks, he'd treated her as if she were made of spun glass.

"Adam," she said for the thousandth time, "you seem to think I've done something extraordinary. I just had a baby."

He leaned over, kissing the tip of her nose. "Wrong, lady. What you did was downright miraculous. You gave me a daughter." Cocking his head, he listened to a muffled protest coming from the next room, then he threw back the covers on his side of the bed, got up and stretched.

Kaylie watched him walk toward the door, magnificently and unself-consciously naked. Every morning he went to claim his daughter and bring her to his wife. Yes, she decided with a wry smile, loincloth or not, there was still an element of Tarzan in Adam. Smiling, she listened to the low-voiced conversation in the other room. Brenna answered with bubbling sounds.

Propping pillows behind her, Kaylie waited for him to come to a stop in the doorway and look at her. Tremendous for the ego, she acknowledged, the way his eyes darkened to near-green and a look somewhere between satisfaction and sheer possessiveness flashed across his face. Some things never changed, though. Adam might have mellowed, he might have found unexpected levels of tenderness in himself, he might even have become a shade more domesticated, but he would never be tamed. And that was just fine with her.

Adam handed Brenna to Kaylie and watched as the baby nuzzled at her breast. There was something primitive and satisfying when a man watched his wife feed their child, he decided. It still had the power to take his breath away.

Three years. It hardly seemed possible. He had never dreamed he could enjoy life so much, laugh so much, love so much. Then, five weeks ago, he'd found that he hadn't even scratched the surface of his feelings. In a small room filled with panting, sweat, loud voices, pain and blood, he had truly learned the meaning of love. Kaylie's hand in his had never seemed so small, her body so fragile. He had never felt so helpless or so terrified.

"When is Opal coming?" Kaylie asked, hoping to remove the shadowy, *remembering* look from his face. Someday, maybe she'd be able to convince him how much strength he had given her, just how much his presence had helped. Maybe.

He grinned, as he always did when she mentioned Opal. Adam was almost as crazy about Opal as he was about his daughter. Of course, it helped that they lived almost six hundred miles apart, and she couldn't choose the most inopportune times to barge in and discuss her plot problems.

"Tomorrow morning. I'll pick her up at the airport about nine."

Opal was coming down for a promotional event one of the bookstores in the mall was sponsoring. Her third book about Edgar had been on the bestseller list for nine weeks.

"Is George surviving the remodeling?"

He nodded. Kaylie had been right. With her talents added to the company, they had sold more "widgets," moved once to larger quarters and were now expanding again.

"Are we going to be at the cabin in time for the fair?"

He nodded again, looking at the shelf that ran high along one wall. It was filled with teddy bears of all sizes and shapes. "This time," he said optimistically, "*I'm* going to win one."

Kaylie smiled. Her smile could still tie him in knots, and probably would as long as there was breath in his body.

"Let's face it, Adam," she said, a clear challenge gleaming in her blue eyes. "You can shoot guns and even hit what you aim at. You can catch robbers. You can terrorize bad guys. But *I* can win teddy bears!"

He leaned over and kissed her laughing mouth.

She sighed. "You sure we have to wait until next week?"

"I'll give you a rain check," he told her.

"Promise?"

He nodded.

Kaylie leaned back with a wicked smile. If she had learned one thing about Adam, it was that he always kept his promises.

* * * * *

*... and now an exciting short story
from Silhouette Books.*

*

HEATHER GRAHAM POZZESSERE
Shadows on the Nile

CHAPTER ONE

Alex could tell that the woman was very nervous. Her fingers were wound tightly about the arm rests, and she had been staring straight ahead since the flight began. Who was she? Why was she flying alone? Why to Egypt? She was a small woman, fine-boned, with classical features and porcelain skin. Her hair was golden blond, and she had blue-gray eyes that were slightly tilted at the corners, giving her a sensual and exotic appeal.

And she smelled divine. He had been sitting there, glancing through the flight magazine, and her scent had reached him, filling him like something rushing through his bloodstream, and before he had looked at her he had known that she would be beautiful.

John was frowning at him. His gaze clearly said that this was not the time for Alex to become interested in a woman. Alex lowered his head, grinning. Nuts to John. He was the one who had made the reservations so late that there was already another passenger between them in their row. Alex couldn't have remained silent anyway; he was certain that he could ease the flight for her.

Besides, he had to know her name, had to see if her eyes would turn silver when she smiled. Even though he should, he couldn't ignore her.

"Alex," John said warningly.

Maybe John was wrong, Alex thought. Maybe this was precisely the right time for him to get involved. A woman would be the perfect shield, in case anyone was interested in his business in Cairo.

The two men should have been sitting next to each other, Jillian decided. She didn't know why she had wound up sandwiched between the two of them, but she couldn't do a thing about it. Frankly, she was far too nervous to do much of anything.

"It's really not so bad," a voice said sympathetically. It came from her right. It was the younger of the two men, the one next to the window. "How about a drink? That might help."

Jillian took a deep, steadying breath, then managed to answer. "Yes . . . please. Thank you."

His fingers curled over hers. Long, very strong fingers, nicely tanned. She had noticed him when she had taken her seat—he was difficult not to notice. There was an arresting quality about him. He had a certain look: high-powered, confident, self-reliant. He was medium tall and medium built, with shoulders that nicely filled out his suit jacket, dark brown eyes, and sandy hair that seemed to defy any effort at combing it. And he had a wonderful voice, deep and compelling. It broke through her fear and actually soothed her. Or perhaps it was the warmth of his hand over hers that did it.

"Your first trip to Egypt?" he asked. She managed a brief nod, but was saved from having to comment when the stewardess came by. Her companion ordered her a white wine, then began to converse with her quite normally, as if unaware that her fear of flying had nearly rendered her speechless. He asked her what she did for a living, and she heard herself tell him that she was a music teacher at a junior college. He responded easily to everything she said, his voice warm and concerned each time he asked another question. She didn't think; she simply answered him, because flying had become easier the moment he touched her. She even told him that she was a widow, that her husband had been killed in a car accident four years ago, and that she was here now to fulfill a long-held dream, because she had always longed to see the pyramids, the Nile and all the ancient wonders Egypt held.

She had loved her husband, Alex thought, watching as pain briefly darkened her eyes. Her voice held a thread of sadness when she mentioned her husband's name. Out of nowhere, he wondered how it would feel to be loved by such a woman.

Alex noticed that even John was listening, commenting on things now and then. How interesting, Alex thought, looking across at his friend and associate.

The stewardess came with the wine. Alex took it for her, chatting casually with the woman as he paid. Charmer, Jillian thought ruefully. She flushed, realizing that it was his charm that had led her to tell him so much about her life.

Her fingers trembled when she took the wineglass. "I'm sorry," she murmured. "I don't really like to fly."

Alex—he had introduced himself as Alex, but without telling her his last name—laughed and said that was the understatement of the year. He pointed out the window to the clear blue sky—an omen of good things to come, he said—then assured her that the airline had an excellent safety record. His friend, the older man with the haggard, world-weary face, eventually introduced himself as John. He joked and tried to reassure her, too, and eventually their efforts paid off. Once she felt a little calmer, she offered to move, so they could converse without her in the way.

Alex tightened his fingers around hers, and she felt the startling warmth in his eyes. His gaze was appreciative and sensual, without being insulting. She felt a rush of sweet heat swirl within her, and she realized with surprise that it was excitement, that she was enjoying his company the way a woman enjoyed the company of a man who attracted her. She had thought she would never feel that way again.

"I wouldn't move for all the gold in ancient Egypt," he said with a grin, "and I doubt that John would, either." He touched her cheek. "I might lose track of you, and I don't even know your name."

"Jillian," she said, meeting his eyes. "Jillian Jacoby."

He repeated her name softly, as if to commit it to memory, then went on to talk about Cairo, the pyramids at Giza, the Valley of the Kings, and the beauty of the nights when the sun set over the desert in a riot of blazing red.

And then the plane was landing. To her amazement, the flight had ended. Once she was on solid ground again, Jillian realized that Alex knew all sorts of things about her, while she didn't know a thing about him or John—not even their full names.

They went through customs together. Jillian was immediately fascinated, in love with the colorful atmosphere of Cairo, and not at all dismayed by the waiting and the bureaucracy. When they finally reached the street she fell head over heels in love with the exotic land. The heat shimmered in the air, and taxi drivers in long burnooses lined up for fares. She could hear the soft singsong of their language, and she was thrilled to realize that the dream she had harbored for so long was finally coming true.

She didn't realize that two men had followed them from the airport to the street. Alex, however, did. He saw the men behind him, and his jaw tightened as he nodded to John to stay put and hurried after Jillian.

"Where are you staying?" he asked her.

"The Hilton," she told him, pleased at his interest. Maybe her dream was going to turn out to have some unexpected aspects.

He whistled for a taxi. Then, as the driver opened the door, Jillian looked up to find Alex staring at her. She felt...something. A fleeting magic raced along her spine, as if she knew what he was about to do. Knew, and should have protested, but couldn't.

Alex slipped his arm around her. One hand fell to her waist, the other cupped her nape, and he kissed her. His mouth was hot, his touch firm, persuasive. She was filled with heat; she trembled...and then she broke away at last, staring at him, the look in her eyes more eloquent than any words. Confused, she turned away and stepped into the taxi. As soon as she was seated she turned to stare after him, but he was already gone, a part of the crowd.

She touched her lips as the taxi sped toward the heart of the city. She shouldn't have allowed the kiss; she barely knew him. But she couldn't forget him.

She was still thinking about him when she reached the Hilton. She checked in quickly, but she was too late to acquire a guide for the day. The manager suggested that she stop by the Kahil bazaar, not far from the hotel. She dropped her bags in her room, then took another taxi to the bazaar. Once again she was enchanted. She loved everything: the noise, the people, the donkey carts that blocked the narrow streets, the shops with their beaded entryways and beautiful wares in silver and stone, copper and brass. Old men smoking water pipes sat on mats drinking tea, while younger men shouted out their wares from stalls and doorways. Jillian began walking slowly, trying to take it all in. She was occasionally jostled, but she kept her hand on her purse and sidestepped quickly. She was just congratulating herself on her competence when she was suddenly dragged into an alley by two Arabs swaddled in burnooses.

"What—" she gasped, but then her voice suddenly fled. The alley was empty and shadowed, and night was coming. One man had a scar on his cheek, and held a long, curved knife; the other carried a switchblade.

"Where is it?" the first demanded.

"Where is what?" she asked frantically.

The one with the scar compressed his lips grimly. He set his knife against her cheek, then stroked the flat side down to her throat. She could feel the deadly coolness of the steel blade.

"Where is it? Tell me now!"

Her knees were trembling, and she tried to find the breath to speak. Suddenly she noticed a shadow emerging from the darkness behind her attackers. She gasped, stunned, as the man drew nearer. It was Alex.

Alex...silent, stealthy, his features taut and grim. Her heart seemed to stop. Had he come to her rescue? Or was he allied with her attackers, there to threaten, even destroy, her?

* * * * *

Watch for Chapter Two of SHADOWS ON THE NILE coming next month—only in Silhouette Intimate Moments.

Silhouette Intimate Moments

Starting in October...

SHADOWS ON THE NILE

by

Heather Graham Pozzessere

A romantic short story in six installments from best-selling author Heather Graham Pozzessere.

The first chapter of this intriguing romance will appear in all Silhouette titles published in October. The remaining five chapters will appear, one per month, in Silhouette Intimate Moments' titles for November through March '88.

Don't miss "*Shadows on the Nile*"—a special treat, coming to you in October. Only from Silhouette Books.

Be There!

Silhouette Romance

COMING NEXT MONTH

#538 TREADMILLS AND PINWHEELS—Glenda Sands
Long ago, Judy Harte had traded the treadmills of ambition for the pinwheels of happiness—but found that there was something missing. Could it be love? J. Hollis Aaron thought so—and he'd trade the key to success for the keys to Judy's heart....

#539 MAIL-ORDER BRIDE—Debbie Macomber
Caroline Myers was furious when she discovered she had been tricked into becoming Paul Trevor's mail-order bride. But Paul's warm eyes soon made her wonder—perhaps he was just what her heart had ordered.

#540 CUPID'S ERROR—Brenda Trent
Opposites attract, but had Cupid blundered by bringing together the wild, impetuous Desha Smith and the conservative, reserved Bryce Gerrard? It might seem like an error, but how could Bryce resist the delicious mischief dancing in Desha's brown eyes?

#541 A TENDER TRAIL—Moyra Tarling
Dress designer April St. Clair had her future all sewn up until famous actor Quinn Quartermain tore back into her life—with danger hot on his trail. Quinn's world was coming apart at the seams—could April's love mend his broken heart?

#542 COMPLIMENTS OF THE GROOM—Kasey Michaels
Amanda Tremaine had everything when she won a dream honeymoon to Atlantic City—except a groom. Free-wheeling Joshua Phillips was willing to oblige her and determined to teach shy Amanda how to take a chance on love....

#543 MADELINE'S SONG—Stella Bagwell
When Madeline Beaumont found she couldn't have a child, she thought the music of love had gone out of her life forever. But then she met tender, infuriating Jake Hunter—could he put a song back in her heart?

AVAILABLE THIS MONTH: Homecoming Celebration!

#532 WOMAN HATER
Diana Palmer

#533 MYSTERY LOVER
Annette Broadrick

#534 THE WINTER HEART
Victoria Glenn

#535 GENTLE PERSUASION
Rita Rainville

#536 OUTBACK NIGHTS
Emilie Richards

#537 FAR FROM OVER
Brittany Young